JOANNA LEE DOSTER

MAXIMUM SPEED

PUSHING THE LIMIT

MPI
PUBLISHING

## COMING SOON

*Maximum Speed: Beyond the Limit*

Cover design, interior book design, and eBook design
by Blue Harvest Creative
*www.blueharvestcreative.com*

Published by
MPI Publishing

ISBN-13: 978-0-9960179-1-6
ISBN-10: 09960179-1-7

Visit the author at:
*www.maximumspeedbook.com*
*www.facebook.com/pages/Maximum-Speed-Pushing-The-Limit/229948400351682*
*www.twitter.com/authorjdoster*
*www.authorjdoster.tumblr.com*

*For my dear and beloved husband, Jeffrey,*
*who is my life, my heart, and my guiding light.*

# ACKNOWLEDGEMENTS

I wish to thank my superb editor, Jeff LaFerney, for his outstanding skills. His remarkable attention to detail, extreme dedication and tireless effort, all helped to keep me "on track."

I wish to acknowledge the following people for their friendship, unwavering support, and invaluable input:

Pat Conner; Mia Amato; Michael Lepp; Jeff Adler; Shane Henty Sutton; Howard Margolis; Scott Morris; Carolyn Guarriello; Geoffrey Ho; Claire and Clifford Huffman; Arlene and Tom Buckley; Chris and Lou Cook; Johnine Cummings; Dr. David Kellman; Jen Grisanti; Mark and Barbara Russell; Rosemarie Brower; Steve and William Reardon; Marsha Casper Cook; Chanel Jennings; Simon Applebaum; Joey Battisti; Megan Richardson; Helen Weber; Ronald A. Williams; Susan and Sander Diamond; Jane, Stephen, Carrie, Sara, and Charles Dossick; Wendy and Peter Bernstein; Rose, Peggy, Christina, and Ron Doster; Diane Vaillancourt; James Klein; Barb Soemann; Elizabeth Wong; Dennis Klein; Nancy Mizels; Bernice and Evan Stone; John Monteleone; Lee and Krissy Landgraver; and Sara and Dennis Belfor.

Honorable mention to:

Blue Harvest Creative Concepts for their creative magic, brilliant designs, and supreme dedication.

Special mention to:

My brother Philip Dossick, who has always inspired me. His genius, love, and talent know no bounds.

Ashley Fontainne, for her infinite wisdom, guidance, and devoted friendship.

Erin Reardon, for her vast knowledge, input and friendship.

Kathy Rosenblatt, for her meticulous research, and unwavering support and friendship.

Marcia Madeira, for her unwavering support, immense talent, and friendship.

Sally J. Walker, for her extraordinary generosity of spirit, friendship, and dedication.

Betty Dravis, for her inspiration, and devoted friendship.

Cyndy Landgraver, for her immense technical knowledge and support.

Henry Chan, for his incredible technical assistance.

Haesook Han, for her great talent, friendship, and extreme dedication.

Retired Detective Richard J. Brower, for his technical assistance.

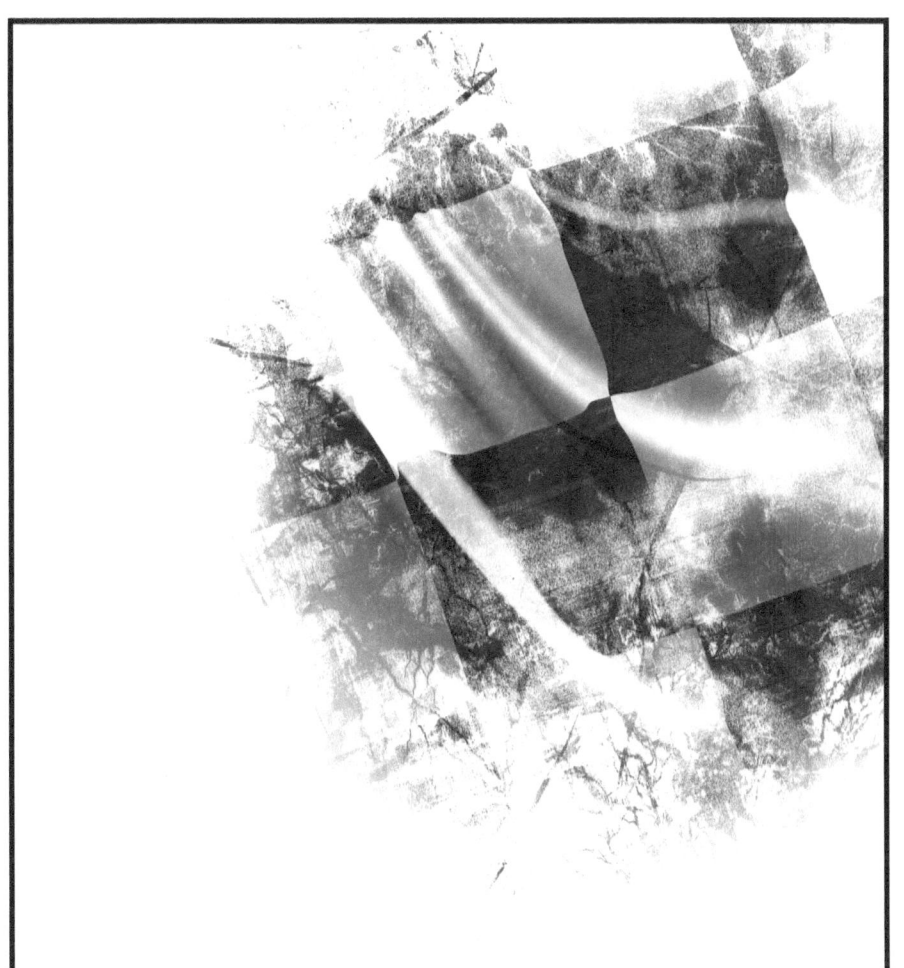

# MAXIMUM SPEED
## PUSHING THE LIMIT

## CHAPTER ONE
# A LIVING DREAM

### SUNDAY MORNING: THE DAY OF THE TRIAX 400 RACE

The heavy raindrops pelted the car's windshield as they came splashing down like rivulets of blood. Sean Devlin was crushed inside and slipping in and out of consciousness. He couldn't move his legs and couldn't see through the crimson-stained windshield. The smell of burnt metal seared right through his senses, and he felt the rhythm of his heartbeat slowing down, just like the race car's dying engine. "D-Dad! ...M-Mom!"

He was finished... never to race again. With a final gasp, he uttered, "Not this."

His piercing scream jolted Daniella Lawson awake. It was the third time that week. Daniella gently shook Sean and tried to soothe him. She nestled her warm body against his and hugged him closely. It was the worst one yet. His nightmares were increasing, and she was sure they had been triggered by the brutal attack he had suffered a few days earlier. "Sean, sweetheart, wake up," she said. "You had another one of your bad dreams." She stroked his hair. "Honey, I'm here. Nothing is going to happen to you!"

Stirring in his dream state, Sean thought he heard something. Was that someone's voice? The words were all muffled, as if someone was speaking from far away. "It's hopeless!" he mumbled.

Still shrouded in terror, he suddenly awoke in a panic, convinced that he was being marked for death. As his fear mounted, he began to agonize over the dangers he and the rest of his team were facing. This wasn't at all like the pranks and horsing around that sometimes went on with competing stock car racing teams or the superstitions some of the professional drivers had, thinking that the next race could be their last. No, this was much worse. Someone was deliberately going after the Devlin Motor Sports (DMS) drivers.

Just a few days before, Sean had been jumped by some thugs who had immobilized him with a taser to his head. Lying on the floor paralyzed, he watched in horror as they kidnapped Jimmy Stanton, his best friend and racing teammate. He was scared out of his mind that things might escalate during the race, and he felt powerless. The only time Sean felt in control of his life was when he was driving a race car. The thrill of speed had always been his lifeline. But this feeling of foreboding was screwing with his head, and he was finding it difficult to stay focused.

Sunrise was coming up fast. He began to go through his mental checklist of what he had to do before the Triax 400, a race that was going to start in a few hours. Working out in the RV's weight room was at the top of the list. He had slept in the Devlin Motor Sports RV near the racetrack, and although he usually stuck to his ironclad rule of not spending the night before any race with girlfriends, rules were meant to be broken, and last night he needed Daniella to be with him, along with his dog, Slate.

Sean rubbed the sleep out of his weary eyes and asked Daniella, who was next to him in bed, "D-d-did I have another one of my death dreams?"

"Yeah, honey, you did! It was a bad one, huh?"

She told him about what he had said in his sleep, and he told her, "That's so weird. I have no memory of it at all. But I d-do have this creeped-out feeling that I can't shake off. Jeez, I'm so burnt out!" He yawned and stretched and then dragged himself out of bed. Once up, he made his way to the weight room and went through his two-hour prerace training routine. It invigorated him, and he felt recharged and ready to get behind the wheel.

Sean was already in the shower when Daniella decided to join him. He was facing away from her when she silently opened the glass door and slipped in behind him. She leaned her supple body into his muscular shoulders and tight butt; wrapping her arms around him, she slowly began caressing him all over.

"Wow, w-who's that? Is that you, Tina?"

"Tina? Who the hell is Tina?"

Daniella was about to push his head under the shower spray in retaliation but thought better of it, not wanting to get his injured head wet. They attempted to get really friendly again but the confining space and very sharp shower handles stopped them cold.

It was time to get dressed and put on his black and gold racing suit. He winced as he brushed his hair, saying, "Ouch...d-d-damn it!" His stitches still hurt like hell. He studied his head in the mirror. Thankfully, the sutures were still holding up, but he was going to have to put his helmet on very carefully.

Ace Devlin, Sean's father, and Sean's older brother, Connor, co-partners in Devlin Motor Sports, were taking all kinds of precautions to fend off any potential surprise attacks before the race. They told Sean to act normal. They had people who had people, who were looking out for him, the other drivers, and crews.

Sean briefly played with Slate and wished he could spend more time with his dog, who he was crazy about. "Who loves you, boy?" he asked, scratching Slate behind his ears one last time for luck. He kissed Daniella hard but had to make a clean break for it or he'd never leave for the racetrack. "See you later, Red," he said.

"Want to scratch me behind my ears for luck?" she asked with a laugh.

Sean smiled at her. "Just think of the great time we'll have celebrating after the race. Later, babe," he called out as he walked out the door.

Ordinarily, he would be jumping out of his skin with excitement, raring to get started. But Jimmy was still nowhere to be found.

"Damn it to hell!" he muttered to himself, worried about his friend.

Jimmy's absence would not go unnoticed by the press and the race fans. Trying to head off any negative publicity, DMS had the track announcer read a statement: *"Due to illness, Jimmy Stanton will not be competing in today's race."* A collective roar of awww's from disappointed fans arose from the stands.

At least the weather was cooperating. There was a pool of light struggling to shine through the hot and hazy thick air of Ormond Beach, Florida. It rained all night, but fortunately it had just stopped.

The thundering roar of the engines, the choking exhaust fumes, and the swell of the crowds suddenly boosted Sean's spirits, and he looked forward to getting back on the track. It was February and twenty-three-year-old Sean Chase Devlin was about to compete in the Triax 400 race, the season opener at Ormond Beach International Speedway. This was going to be his third year as the defending Pro Motorsports Racing Association (PMRA) champion, having won the past two seasons.

He had just left the Devlin Motor Sports garage. With a quick high-five to his crew chief, Billy Ray Harper, he waved to Daniella and his family in their team's pit box. Sean stopped to sign a few autographs for the fans, smiling as he took in the whole scene. Getting caught up in the moment, he sighed and thought, *God, it can't get better than this.*

Sean eased his lanky, five-foot, ten-inch body into his black and gold #17 Chevy. He signaled to one of his crew assistants that he needed help putting on his helmet. The kid placed it carefully over his head, keeping clear of the bandage. Sean fastened his seat harness into place, clicked the steering wheel to the column, and checked the connections for the two-way radio in his helmet.

Finally, the announcer called, "Drivers, start your engines!" Sean turned on the power switch and flipped the ignition switch with his thumb. The #17 car roared to life. Black exhaust smoke billowed over the car. He revved the engine a few times to feel the power.

He always had one vision, and that was to be a great racer. He didn't put much thought into the ultimate physical challenges his body was about to endure, sweltering in one hundred twenty degree temperatures inside his car's cockpit, with little relief. He had to tough it out, breathing in the smoke and carbon monoxide fumes flowing back into the car. And if that wasn't enough, he needed Olympian strength to withstand the two to three G forces while driving the two ton car, squeezed into a cramped, custom-fitted bucket seat for hours on end.

He suddenly snapped to attention and spoke into his helmet radio, saying in his usual easygoing manner, "Hey, let's get going, Billy Boy." Sean was always able to block out the other forty-two cars revving up and never worried about competition. He had learned how to focus from Taylor Devlin, his mother, a former stock car racer, who first taught him to drive when he was nine years old.

He kept his blue-green eyes fixed on the track in front of him. His helmet's visor would protect him from the scorching and blinding sun that would be his companion for the next several hours.

The rumbling pack of forty-three cars followed the pace car around the track. As the pace car veered off the track, the cheering crowd jumped to its feet, only to be drowned out by the deafening roar of the engines as the green flag came waving down. A mad cluster of cars jammed into the first turn of the four hundred mile race. Already the agonizing crunch of metal against metal signaled the start of the battle for victory lane.

"Aaaand they're off," Billy Ray said into his headset mic. "Sean, no ramming and jamming today, okay?" He was referring to the past year's bumps and fights with other drivers.

"Roger that!" Sean replied with a laugh into the helmet radio.

The track surface started to heat up, and lap after lap Sean was fighting with the car to avoid fishtailing or sliding into the wall. He was doing his best to hold his lead, but the other cars kept crowding him. He had no choice but to let up on the power to keep the car under control. "Hey Billy Boy, the right front tire feels loose, okay?"

"Ten-four," said Billy Ray. "Pit stop coming up shortly."

Still in the lead position, Sean glanced in his rearview mirror. Buzzy Durant in car #22 and Joey Packer in the #34 car were battling for position behind Dakota Philips, Sean's DMS teammate in car #23, who was a car length behind the speedier Carl Zimmer, #41, star driver of Villereal/Clayton Racing for the past ten years and Sean's hero since he was a kid hanging out in his grandfather's garage in North Carolina. Sean's grandfather Taylor Clayton Sr. co-owned Villereal/ Clayton Racing with Benecio Villereal.

Confident he could take the lead from Sean, Carl Zimmer moved up fast in the outside lane on Sean's right. Sean reacted by speeding up into the turn. Billy Ray said to Sean over the radio, "Take it easy, Sean, let the #41 car pass—don't be hasty, boy. See what Zimmer does with the sharp curve, and don't make him nervous." Zimmer's tires smoked as he dove into the curve too fast. Sean chuckled to himself as he regained the lead from Zimmer, who lost his momentum. "Billy Boy," he said, "you are good!" The crew chief, standing at his perch on pit road, crossed his arms and quietly smirked.

Three hours into the race, the distinctive swirl marks of somebody else's wheel coming in contact with the right side of Sean's car had nearly wiped off his bright red number 17 down to the sheet metal. There was Carl Zimmer getting caught in the middle, as Dakota Philips wedged her way on the outside lane, running three cars wide where there was only room enough for two cars and change. They were all speeding past a slower car that was hugging the yellow line on the inside lane, and there was nowhere to go. *Wham!* "Jeez!" Sean shouted as he felt his tires break loose and his car began to skid uncontrollably.

"But wait, folks," said the track announcer. "Sean Devlin is not out of this three-way challenge yet! He's getting his car out of the slide! Look out, Carl Zimmer and Dakota Philips! This ain't over...."

Sean kept working the steering wheel to steady the car. Downshifting, he pumped the clutch pedal and jammed the gearshift forward, determined to retake the lead. He dove down to pass Zimmer on the inside lane, or so he thought. Billy Ray's voice crackled over the radio in Sean's helmet, trying his best to hide his anger. "Sean, you've been penalized for passing below the yellow line. Bring it in. You have to take a pass through the pits. And for God's sake, remember to watch the speed limit."

"Black flagged? Fuck! Fuck this shit! That #41 car forced me off the track! Didn't they see that?"

Billy Ray, sensing that Sean was growing more flustered, tried to calm him. "Forget it, Sean. Take a deep breath and get your head straight. The race ain't over and the fat lady hasn't sung. We still have time to catch them."

Sean was still grumbling about relinquishing his lead to serve a pass-through penalty when another caution flag came out. Debris on the track in turn three blew out a tire on car #15, which spun out in a cloud of smoke. The fans saw car #15's exhaust pipe spew out a huge orange flame as the driver cranked the motor up. They cheered him on as his #15 car limped past the stands on its way back to the pit for new tires. Sean also pitted for a change of tires, and then caught up to the back of the pack.

The track was cleared for a restart once again. Sean's #17 car stuck tight to the track as he worked his way through the slower cars and made his way back to Zimmer at the front of the pack. Sean's car responded to every maneuver and gained ground with every lap. With the patience of a seasoned pro, along with having a very fast car; it was only a matter of time before he had his chance to retake the lead. He had to get past the remaining top five cars in the race. He soon passed Dakota Philips to reach second position. Finally in striking distance to retake the lead from Carl Zimmer, Sean maneuvered in such a way that he was bumper to bumper with him. He drafted the #41 car in preparation to slingshot his way around Zimmer and into the lead.

Zimmer was ready for him and tried to block Sean's passing move. Choosing the right moment, Sean turned his wheel and tromped on the accelerator when, within a split second, his car bucked, striking the back of Zimmer's car, which fishtailed. Sean's car backfired a fiery explosion that sounded like a blast of a cannon round. His rear wheels locked up, causing the speeding car to violently swerve to the right and smash into the wall with such ferocity that it catapulted into the air. In a matter of seconds, Sean's car crash-landed, rolled over a few times, and careened into Zimmer's car, which caused Zimmer to spin sideways under a cloud of tire smoke. Zimmer crashed into another car as the rest of the pack scattered to avoid the crash, ducking left and right.

"W-what the hell is happening, Billy?" Sean screamed, now dizzy and disoriented. He kept hearing more crashing and crumbling metal. The world was a spinning blur before him as the remains of his #17 car tossed end over end, bits and pieces of metal flying in every direction.

Voices...he heard voices, familiar voices. He heard Billy Ray's voice saying, "Sean! Oh my God! Sean, can you hear me?" Other voices were yelling, "Get the damn ambulance!" "What th—unhh..."

Sean was barely conscious. *Holy Jesus!* His death dream was coming true! Everything turned dark, and his head felt like it was being gripped in a vise. He heard himself yell, "Billy, get me outta here!" *Pain.* His left leg was badly bruised and aching too. His body felt like it was being stretched on a pulley. He smelled smoke and leaking engine coolant. He could hear footsteps shuffling around the car. Fire extinguishers quelled the remaining flames. Men were shouting to each other and pulled hard on his body. He was being dragged out of the car. He heard ambulance sirens. Then, silence. Sean passed out.

## CHAPTER TWO
# IN HIS BROTHER'S SHADOW

### MONDAY: THE MORNING AFTER THE TRIAX 400 RACE

The private hospital room was dark except for a harsh light on the wall above his bed. Sean awoke disoriented and panicked in the strange surroundings. "Muh-M-Mom—what's going...? W-where am I?" He heard a soothing, familiar voice.

Sean tried to clear his head and then heard, "Top of the wee hours of the morning to you, Sean. You're in Ormond Beach General Hospital. It's me, Dr. Schottstein, your good ole reliable doctor, who always manages to put you back together."

Still a bit confused, Sean panicked again and cried out, "W-what happened? O-oh, please—my head."

"Calm yourself, son," said Dr. Schottstein. "You're lucky to be alive. You sustained a slight concussion and really banged up your knee. You were in a car crash. Do you remember racing yesterday?"

"Umm, yeah, yeah, Doc, I remember. *Oww*! Jeez, I feel like a punching b-bag. And my h-head aches."

"Well, we can do something about that, Sean. I want you to rest up. I'm going to give you something to let you sleep and take away your pain." The doctor administered the meds, and Sean very quickly drifted off peacefully.

When he awoke again a few hours later, he still felt shaky. He slowly opened his eyes and saw his whole family standing around him;

he gasped as he tried to blink back his tears. "Oh God," he blurted out. "I am so s-s-sorry. It wasn't supposed to turn out this way." He knew that he was causing them to relive the horrible memories of his oldest brother's crash, five years earlier.

Connor, who was the first in his family to become a PMRA racing champion, had crashed in the Gator 500 back then and was lucky to get out alive. His accident was very similar to Sean's crash, but Connor, after sustaining a badly crushed leg, was left with a hobbling limp and never raced again. After his near-fatal crash, Connor made a new life for himself as a successful businessman in New York City.

"D-D-Dad, I'm so sorry I tore up the car. I could have won that race! And now..." He started sobbing. "I'm making you go through h-hell all over again. I can't stand it!"

Daniella, his girl, and Avery, his twin sister, sat on either side of him in his bed and put their arms around Sean, hugging him tightly. Connor came over and put his hand on Sean's shoulder. Sean's father, tearing up, said in his Boston accent, "Son, stop this blaming yourself. We are just happy to see you alive. To hell with the race cah. That can be replaced." His voice cracked with emotion.

Sean's mother, Taylor, in an uncharacteristic move, ran over to her son and pushed everyone aside; she held him in her arms, rocking him softly and cooing in her southern lilt, "Honee...honee, everything is all right. Ya'll just rest up and get better."

His friends, crew chief Billy Ray Harper and Hank Cho, were waiting to see Sean. They were trying to put up a good front and not break down, but the distraught look on their faces gave them away. Most of the guys from Devlin Motor Sports were taking turns hanging around in the hospital hallways, pacing and nervously waiting for an update on Sean's status.

Members of the press were also waiting, hungry for headlines. Ace persuaded his colleagues in the media to keep a lid on the story temporarily, but he knew he couldn't keep it under wraps for long.

Sean looked out the window in his room and said, "What d-d-day is it?"

Ace answered, "It's Monday, son."

Sean suddenly remembered that Jimmy was missing; he had been kidnapped three days before and missed Sunday's race. Sean asked, "Where's Jimmy? Have you found him yet, Dad?"

When Ace shook his head, Sean beat his fist into his hand with worry and confusion. Connor said, "Don't worry, bro, we'll find him. And then we'll kick his ass for making us all worry about him."

Sean reached down to touch the cast on his left leg and cried out, "Agh!" wincing with more pain. His meds were messing with his head. Memories of Connor's crash kept flooding back in, forcing Sean to remember how everyone had sat frozen in their seats, barely breathing until they heard that his brother was alive and being airlifted to the hospital. He was so confused. Or did that happen to him in yesterday's crash?

Sean kept blinking his eyes as if to make sure that what was happening was real and in the present. Dr. Schottstein looked over at him and gave him a reassuring smile. The doctor's beeper suddenly went off, making everyone in the room jump. With that, Dr. Schottstein scooted over to Sean's bedside and whispered to him calmly, "Son, just buzz me if you need anything, and listen: try and chill out, okay? Your family just wants to spend time with you. They've been so worried, so don't start with that heavy self-blame guilt trip. Leave *that* to my mother!"

Just then Dakota Philips, nicknamed "Phil," strolled into the room. All heads turned to look at her, particularly Daniella's. Sean's heart began to pound a million times faster as it always did when he saw the tall, striking, dark haired beauty. She was Billy Ray's live-in girlfriend and had been driving for DMS a few years longer than Sean. She was gaining a reputation as one of the top drivers on the Pro Motorsports Racing Association circuit. "Hey, everybody...Hi, Sean," she said with a million dollar smile that melted hearts.

Sean grunted, "Hey, Phil."

"Glad to see you're in one piece," she said, while looping her arm through Billy Ray's. She turned to the group and whispered, "Did you tell him?"

Suddenly the room became deadly still, as if all the air had been sucked out of it. Sean heard his father whispering, "Look Dakota, maybe this isn't the time or place."

"Tell me what? W-what's going on? Hey, what are you all w-whispering about? W-will someone please fill me in?"

Sean held his head up, trying to make eye contact with his father, Ace, who said, "Son, Dakota won the race yesterday."

Sean, reeling from gut-wrenching disappointment as well as the pain, closed his eyes and pressed his bedside button for more medication; sleep would be welcoming.

## CHAPTER THREE

# WHAT'S GOING ON?

As Ace, Connor, and the rest of the family were leaving the hospital, Connor pulled his father aside to speak with him privately. He looked around to make sure they were alone, and in a hushed voice said to Ace, "Dad, I have even more bad news. PMRA disqualified Sean from the Triax race after his car failed the PMRA post inspection. The officials said they found questionable programming in the car's computer and there is evidence of flash drive tampering. They said that under the circumstances they have no choice but to disqualify Sean pending further investigation."

Ace was seething with anger. "Jesus *Christ*! First Jimmy disappears, then Sean crashes his cah, now PMRA is accusing us of tampering? This is insane! Didn't anybody check that computer before the race?"

Connor lowered his voice, "Billy Ray said they didn't find anything out of place prior to the race. He said they checked and rechecked that car. It even passed PMRA's prerace inspection."

Ace was puzzled. "But we didn't do anything wrong, son. None of this makes sense. Sean was almost killed for God's sake."

"I know, Dad. But all the settings on the computer were different when they checked it after the crash. They think we might have altered the programming to win the race."

"Connah that computer was PMRA specific."

"Well, Dad, they said it wasn't."

Ace paused to think. Then his face brightened slightly. "You know, son, something's not right heah and we are not going to take this without fighting back! File a protest with PMRA. Let's have Hank investigate. This nonsense smacks of sabotage to me."

"Okay Dad, I'll make the calls and have him get on it immediately."

Ace stroked his hair back in disbelief, thinking, *Someone is targeting us and causing all of these disasters. But who?*

He turned to Connor and said, "Well, at least Dakota won the race. They can't take that away from us."

Connor grimaced, "Yeah, well, they impounded her car. They haven't found anything wrong yet, but they are going over it with a fine-tooth comb."

## CHAPTER FOUR
# *REWIND*

### *FRIDAY: TWO DAYS BEFORE THE TRIAX 400*

The soft light from the early morning rays was sifting through the shutters of Sean's forty foot RV which sat on a quiet cul-de-sac in Ormond Beach. Long shadows revealed the wreckage from the party the night before. Empty beer bottles cluttered the galley kitchen table. A few more were lying on the beer-stained floor. The automatic coffeemaker blinked on, and soon the aroma of fresh brew wafted over the stench of stale beer.

Sean woke up in his king-sized bed and found a very slender, nude young girl, barely stirring in her sleep, lying next to him. The disheveled sheets had fallen onto the floor. "Holy crap!" he said. For a moment, he couldn't remember where he had met this one. *Oh yeah*, he recalled. *It was last night at Tito's Bar.* Sean was spoiled; being one of the hottest race car drivers around had its rewards. Women were always throwing themselves at him. He had his pick every night. His fooling around was what ruined his relationship with Daniella. For the most part, every stray girl or fan he slept with now was just a poor substitute for Daniella Lawson and Dakota Philips, his fantasy lust who was totally unavailable and not the least bit interested in him.

The pretty girl rolled over and nudged him. Sean, not being able to resist her, went at it one more time. She moaned with ecstasy and clung to him, wanting more.

A little while later, the girl got up and heard running water through the bathroom door. Sean was splashing water on his face, struggling to revive himself after a heavy night of partying. "Crap," he said into the mirror. "How the hell am I going to get rid of her?"

The girl was now sitting on the edge of the bed, pushing her long silky blond hair out of her slender face, slightly freckled from the previous day's bright sun. Her tan lines accentuated her perky breasts and a pierced navel. "Uhh...coffee...I smell coffee," the pretty girl mumbled, still hung over from the night before.

Sean came out of the bathroom and stuttered, "W-w-what's your name again? Never mind. Please, you g-gotta get outta here...now! I don't w-want anybody to see you here. Get d-dressed!"

Just then, he heard Jimmy "JP" Stanton's Camaro rumble to a stop outside the RV. As Sean's best friend and racing teammate stepped out of his sleek muscle car, he could hear voices inside the RV. To be a real pain to Sean, Jimmy began banging on the sides of the RV over and over again, as he laughed his butt off.

"Yeah, yeah, I'm up. Jeez! Knock it off, will ya? You sonuva..." Sean reached for the entry door to let Jimmy in. "What's up?" was as close to a cheery greeting as Sean could muster.

Jimmy smirked, "What's up, Devlin!" Sean automatically flipped him the bird. Jimmy looked at Sean, who was still in his boxers, and asked, "Ain't you ready yet?"

Sean made some guttural sounds as he fumbled around for his favorite coffee mug and tossed its cruddy contents into the kitchen sink.

Jimmy, hearing a noise from the back of the RV, looked over Sean's shoulder and saw the nude girl. As she was about to treat herself to a satisfying yawn, she raised her sleepy eyes and realized she had an audience. Suddenly aware of her nakedness, she blushed as she scrambled to throw a sheet around herself.

Jimmy turned to Sean and raised an eyebrow, asking, "Who's your friend?"

Sean struggled to pull his pants on while jumping around on one foot. In his haste, he stumbled over himself and crashed into the wall. "Dammit! *Argh!*"

Jimmy ducked out of the way as Sean bounced off the wall. As he dodged his off-balanced teammate, Jimmy turned to Sean and said while laughing, "Walk much?"

The girl, still wrapped in a bed sheet, ambled into the kitchen and filled a semi-clean mug with hot coffee; she giggled sweetly and asked, "Does this happen every morning?"

Sean laughed, "Yes!"

As she turned and walked away, she spotted his motorcycle helmet on the couch. She could feel their eyes on her bare butt as she slowly leaned over the couch; she lingered a few extra seconds before grabbing Sean's helmet and tossing it to him.

She said, giggling, "You should wear this when you get dressed in the morning. It's safer."

Jimmy guffawed while choking on his coffee. Sean stood with his pants around his ankles and glared at the girl as she walked away, letting the bed sheet slide off her shoulder, exposing all of her sweet assets. "C-c'mon, get d-dressed. You g-gotta go," he said, annoyed with himself for still being attracted to her.

Jimmy said, "Come on Sean, get ready. We have to get to the garage. Billy Ray told me to get you to the track on time for a change." Just then, the girl walked out of the bedroom fully dressed.

"I will," Sean said as he winked at her, "just as s-soon as I throw out the t-trash."

"You SOB!" she shouted.

Without warning, she jumped on top of Sean and punched him.

"Hey, owww! I was just joking," laughed Sean.

Sean patted the girl's butt, as he shoved her out the door, and said, "Thanks for a great t-time blondie." Jimmy was sore from laughing so hard.

The door slammed shut. Sean and Jimmy picked up their coffee mugs and clinked them together in a toast of brotherhood.

## CHAPTER FIVE
# *GOING A.W.O.L.*

The Ormond Beach sky was turning fiery red as dusk approached. Sean, Jimmy, Dakota, and the rest of the Devlin Motor Sports staff were listening to the final points of the data analysis wrap-up, after their all-day practice and racing trials. Knowing that their long day was about to come to an end, the three drivers started to pack up and get ready to leave the company RV. They had worked hard to prepare for the most prestigious race of the season, the Gator 500, which was the following Saturday, a week after the Triax. It was critical for DMS to win at the Gator and take home the trophy.

Winning the Triax would be a nice bonus, but DMS was mainly interested in working out all the kinks for the big race. It was a given that each driver's crew would be working on their cars around the clock. The cars were all about evenly matched, so the difference between winning or losing a race would be in the hands of the drivers and their crews.

The meeting over, the young drivers began to think about their plans for the evening. Sean turned around to face his friends.

"Hey guys, what are you all doing tonight?"

Jimmy's face brightened as he was about to make a suggestion, but Dakota spoke up first.

26

"I'm kinda tired tonight, fellas. How 'bout a rain check?"

"No prob, Phil. Rest up! We'll have some serious partyin' to do after the Gator!" Sean grinned and winked.

"Yeah...right. See you guys tomorrow." Dakota brushed her long, dark hair aside in the breeze and watched the boys walk away.

As Sean and Jimmy left the garage area, they had to walk along the long fence that was keeping the hundreds of fans at bay, all craning their necks to get a glimpse of the drivers coming out of the gate.

The two DMS drivers waved to the fans, who were screaming, "Sean! Oh, Sean! Hey, Jimmy Stanton! Hey guys! Come over here! Can we have your autograph?" A group of girls shouted, "Look over here!" as they blatantly eyeballed the boys in their skin-tight racing pants and windbreakers. Sean and Jimmy walked over to the gate and began signing autographs and talking to the cheering fans who presented T-shirts and caps to be autographed by their favorite drivers. A starry-eyed eight-year-old boy and his father approached Sean, holding out a pen and a poster of Sean posing in front of his #17 car.

"C-c-c...C-c-can I h-h-h..."

Sean had a childhood flashback, remembering his own painful stutter, and said quickly, to spare the boy any embarrassment, "Hey champ!" He snatched the pen out of the boy's hand and presented his own hand in a genuine handshake. "I'm Sean Devlin. What's your name?"

"T-Tommy."

"Well, Tommy, I'm very glad to meet you!" said Sean. "Here for the Triax 400 race this Sunday?"

"Yup!" said Tommy.

"Are you coming to the Gator 500 next Saturday?"

The boy grinned and said, "You b-b-bet, Sean! And I'm c-c-coming to see you win!"

Sean smiled and signed the poster. Tommy's dad spoke up, pointing to his camera. "D'ya mind?"

"No prob! Here, Tommy, smile," he said as he kneeled next to the boy. Afterward, Sean shook Tommy's father's hand and said, "He's a great kid!"

Tommy's dad thanked Sean and took his son's hand. "C'mon, Tommy. Let's go!"

Sean overheard Tommy shouting to his dad, "W-wow Dad! Did you s-see *that*? Sh-Sh-Sean Devlin sh-shook m-m*y* hand!"

Jimmy and Sean grinned at each other. Jimmy said, "Way to go, bro."

"Okay folks, we gotta get going. See y'all at the races." Sean turned to look at Jimmy. His expression changed, and he said in a more agitated tone, "Hey, JP, I have to b-blow off s-steam. Let's b-beat it out of here and g-go see Avery in South Beach." Jimmy knew that Sean's nervousness often aggravated his stuttering. Sean was still pining away for Daniella Lawson, who had broken up with him the year before. Daniella had been hired by Sean's brother, Connor, a few years back, to do marketing and PR for his two very popular night clubs in South Beach, and Avery, Sean's twin sister, managed both of them. The girls lived in apartments at the Hotel Escondido in South Beach. Jimmy smiled at the prospect of seeing Avery, who he had been in love with since they were kids. The four of them—Sean, Jimmy, Avery, and Daniella—used to hang out together with their friends at the coolest nightclubs.

Sean got out his phone and texted Avery.

Hey, Sis! JP and I will be in South Beach 2 nite. Book us 2 rooms @ hotel.

She texted him right back, saying, Gr8 bro no prob. Can't wait 2 CU!

## CHAPTER SIX
# ROAD TRIP TO SOUTH BEACH

### EARLY FRIDAY EVENING: TWO DAYS BEFORE THE TRIAX RACE

South Beach was about two and a half hours from Ormond Beach for most drivers, but Sean's need for speed would make short work of the trip. He decided to get his electric-blue 1967 Corvette out of the private garage near the Devlins' condo along Ormond Beach. Sean kept a few classic cars stashed around his favorite haunts and the family holdings.

The Vette was an icon of its era, with the sleek fiberglass Sting Ray body and the bright chromeplated side exhaust pipes adorning the rocker panels. Sean loved the throaty sound of the exhaust and the quick response the Chevy engine delivered. With the tricked-out blue paint job, heads were guaranteed to turn. Even though it wasn't one of his fastest cars, Sean loved that Vette.

Jimmy hopped over the passenger door and glided his skinny butt into the bucket seat. Strapping himself in, he shouted, "Let's go!" With that, Sean shifted into first gear and hit the gas. Both boys grinned with satisfaction as Sean worked the gears, chirping the tires on each shift. Sean turned to Jimmy and said, "You're in charge of tunes."

Jimmy looked at the dashboard and said, "Hey, what happened to the radio?"

"I had things upgraded. Wait 'til you get a load of the new sound system I had put in!"

"Oh yeah? What's that for?" Jimmy said, pointing to a new USB port in the dashboard.

"Check it out! Get the memory stick out of the console and plug it in," Sean said.

"You set this rod up for digital music? Sw-eet!" Jimmy shouted as he plugged in the stick. The music rocked the inside of the car, and Jimmy yelled, "Hot damn, this is awesome!"

Sean laughed out loud and punched the accelerator. The Vette growled and roared down the highway, as its taillights faded to tiny red dots. At least that was how it looked to the sedan that was following behind them. He'd seen enough. On went his red and blue lights. Their trip to South Beach was about to be delayed.

Trooper Earl Hammond was already working himself into a lather as he approached the sports car. "Who does this smart-ass think he is, driving like a maniac on my beat?" he muttered while adjusting his Stetson hat. Composing himself, he shined the flashlight on the driver, then the passenger, and then again on the driver.

"Sean Devlin? Jimmy Stanton! What are you guys up to?"

Sean looked through his open window at the rugged features of the cop.

"Oh my God; hey Hamm! How the hell are you? You working this drag tonight?"

The trooper grinned and said, "Yeah, and look who I snared. A couple of race car jockeys. Forget you aren't at the track, Devlin?"

"Well, you know me, Earl. Can't be number two, on the track or off. In fact, if I wasn't testing my brakes, you'd never have caught up to me in that so-called Interceptor," Sean said, laughing and pointing back to the police cruiser parked behind him.

"Watch it, son. I got more horses under the hood than this antique go-kart," Trooper Hammond said, trying awfully hard to be deadly seriousness.

Sean threw the trooper another verbal jab and asked, "So you gonna bust me?"

"Y'all think you can behave yerselves tonight?" said Hammond.

"Naturally!" Sean said, turning to his buddy, grinning. "Right, JP?"

Jimmy piped up, "Uh, yeah, sure!"

"You guys racing the Gator?"

"We'll be there, Hamm," said Sean.

"Okay boys, don't ferget, y'all owe me an autograph for the kids. And don't make me be lookin' fer ya. Now, y'all take it easy, you heah?" said Hammond.

"Okay Earl. Thanks. See ya!" Sean shouted over his shoulder as he rolled away. "Jimmy! Hit the tunes!"

Trooper Hammond stood with his hands on his hips, watching as Sean jammed it into second gear. As he turned and walked back to the cruiser, he slowly shook his head and smirked while muttering, "Damn those boys."

## CHAPTER SEVEN
## CONNOR AND
## THE TWINS

### DETOUR TO SOUTH BEACH BEFORE THE RACE

Sean called his brother, Connor, who was working in his Wall Street investment firm. "Hey Connor," said Sean over the car phone. "It's me and Jimmy. How are you, bro? Freezing your ass off up there in New York City?"

"Hey, Sean! Hi, Jimmy! Yeah, it's cold. We're good. The baby is keeping us up all night, but it's okay!"

"Can't wait to meet the little fella and see you guys too! Give Genji my best."

"Sure will. So what's up, Sean? Isn't the Triax race this Sunday?"

"Yeah, but we're taking the Vette to see Avery in South Beach; we'll hang out overnight and then come back and kick butt at the race."

"Aren't you cutting it close, Sean? You know we're all flying in tomorrow night for it."

"Well, I just need to blow off some steam; I promise to be back at the track in time."

"Okay, don't worry; I won't blow your cover to the old man."

"Thanks, bro. Oh, anything you want me to tell Avery?"

"No thanks. She's about to call me any minute now for our weekly phone meeting."

"All right, Connor. See you all on Sunday."

"Bye, bro. Have fun."

"Right....See ya!" said Sean.

Connor, twenty-eight years old, and the best looking of the Devlin family, was over six feet two, a few inches taller than Ace. He had perfect features—a great jawline, jet-black hair, and deep brown eyes—but it was his deep voice that was hypnotizing. His pronounced limp was the only thing that detracted from his good looks.

Just then, Avery phoned him from her South Beach office.

"Hey, Connor! How you guys doing in snowy New York? And how's my cute little nephew Thomas?"

Hi, Sis. The baby is teething, but still a little trooper, Genji and I are fine, thanks.

Just heard from Sean. He and Jimmy are on their way to see you now."

"Yeah, Sean just texted me. It'll be great to see him. I'm gonna throw them a party."

"Avery, do me a favor please and make sure the boys are back in time for the big race on Sunday. We're all going to be there, remember?"

Avery laughed. "Don't worry about Sean! He'll make it back; he always does. He's still missing Daniella and wants to reconnect with her. Make you a bet on that."

"I know; you're right, little sister."

"So Connor, you ready? I got my weekly numbers from the clubs for you!" Avery proudly announced that Club Sucre and Club Bezo had turned a profit for the sixth month in a row. Connor reflected on her tremendous success. In the past three years as manager, she had turned his two South Beach nightclubs into the hottest ones around and the most profitable!

Connor remembered back to when Avery was having a hard time with drugs and alcohol and was fighting for her life in rehab. She had the reputation of being a notorious party girl, and there were often blurbs about her in Page Six of the New York Post, on TV tabloid shows, and in gossip magazines; people were always drawn to her. Connor knew that if she had a focus—and an opportunity—she'd succeed. He gave her both, and she proved him right.

"Well, Sis, I gotta hand it to you! You're blowing everybody out of the water and you're only twenty-three! The numbers look great. I am so proud of you!"

"Thanks, Connor! You don't know how much I appreciate that. You believed in me before I believed in myself. I never want to disappoint you." Avery was so touched by what her brother had said, she began to cry.

Connor heard his sister put down her cell phone and take a sip of water to regain her composure. After she was came back on the line, he said, "I guess we are all survivors in our own way. Remember when my racing career ended five years ago?"

"Yes," she said.

"It was hard for me to come to grips with my bad leg," said Connor. "Coming from our family, you know how it is with Mom: 'One cannot have any handicaps.' Thank goodness we have Dad, who happens to be the most incredible man, despite being our father. He always said, 'Connah, my son, there ah two types of people in life—one who looks in the mirrah and sees every flaw and imperfection, and the other type who looks in the mirrah and says *I'm terrific!* It's bettah to be like the second fella. Then you can focus on the real things in life! It's bettah anyway in business to feel and act confident, even if you're not, because that will make the other fella feel uneasy.'"

Avery said, "We are so lucky to have him as our dad. What the hell did he see in our mother?"

They both chuckled knowingly.

She said to Connor, "Mother was so hard to please. You know the hell I'd been through getting over my addictions. But you can't imagine the living hell Sean had to endure with his childhood stutter."

"What are you talking about, Avery?"

Avery sighed. "Hey bro, when you were away at military school you missed a lot of stuff. I never told you that I used to get into a lot of fist fights with the jerks in the neighborhood who would mock and imitate Sean's stutter. Nobody else would defend him. Forget Mother. She was part of the problem. She was impossible to be around whenever she ridiculed him. I *hated* it! I wanted so much to punch her out for picking on Sean. He was a tough kid, though. He would hide his feelings from Mother and cry when he was alone."

"Holy crap, Avery! I had no idea the hell Mom put Sean through."

Avery switched hands with her phone and wiped the tears from her face. She composed herself and continued, "Mom tried a lot of so-called *cures* to get him to stop stuttering. She dragged him to the best speech therapists all over the city. It might have worked eventually, but she wanted instant results. She wanted them to *fix* Sean. The poor kid was under so much pressure to be perfect."

Connor related to that instantly. He said, "Yeah, I know. Mom couldn't tolerate any weaknesses in herself, and God help anyone else who didn't measure up. Dad once told me Mom was so hard on us because that was the way Grandpa Clayton raised her after Grandma Mariella died."

Avery said, "Poor sweet Grandma Mariella died so young. Jeez, Mom was only ten years old at the time. I still remember how some relatives would shush me up if I mentioned Grandma's name or asked a question about her. Mother would get all stony quiet. Grandma's death must have really affected Mom more deeply than she ever let on."

The two of them liked to reminisce whenever they could, even when they were on the phone. When Sean joined in, it was like family group therapy sessions and gave them a chance to go over unfinished stuff.

Avery continued, "Speaking of nutcases, I remember when Mother was going to try another one of her fixes on Sean. We were living in our apartment in New York City. It was the night before our ninth birthday. Our nanny, Consuela, told me that Mother had bought me—now get this, Con—a boy's ten-speed bike for my birthday, despite knowing how desperately I wanted to take ballet lessons. Mother told me repeatedly, 'Honee, you're too tall and too plump. I wouldn't want you to embarrass yourself in public.'"

Connor said, "No, she didn't say that, did she? Really?"

"Oh yeah!"

"Now that is wicked! But of course, that's our mom."

"But wait, it gets better," Avery continued. "I heard Mother's footsteps walk past my room into Sean's bedroom to wake him up in the middle of the night. You should have heard Sean squealing in protest. Jeez, the kid was sound asleep."

"Next thing I knew, Connor, I heard her drag Sean downstairs. I secretly followed them in another elevator as Mother took Sean down to the apartment building's enormous basement garage, and saw her plunk him into the front seat of her sports car."

"What the hell was she doing?"

"I guess she was going to teach Sean how to drive. No, actually, she had something else going on in that twisted mind of hers."

Connor laughed.

Avery continued, "Sean later told me he was kind of thrilled to be in her car and had been sneaking down to make believe he was a racer. Guess Mom found out from Jafar, the all-night garage attendant, and figured it would be a good time to test how brave Sean was. She figured she would pass down the family business to her speed-crazy son. Did she ever do that to you, Connor?"

"She tried, but since I am almost six years older than you two, she at least waited until my feet could reach the pedals."

Avery snorted out a laugh. "Mother convinced herself that teaching Sean to drive would give him something to be confident about—pedal to the metal and all that bullshit she got into when she was racing stock cars for Grandpa. Her real reason for taking Sean down to the garage in the middle of the night was to cure him. Make him a perfect child. Mother had this idea that if Sean became addicted to the thrill of speed and car racing, it would somehow distract him from his stuttering. Poor Sean squirmed and rubbed his eyes to shake off sleep as Mother showed him how to put his feet on the pedals, hands on the steering wheel, and then, *Jesus Christ*, she let him drive around in the garage."

"Now that is wacked! I think I would have completely bailed! Wow!"

"Yeah, I was scared for Sean. I was holding my breath, but Sean was getting into it! He forgot about his nervousness and instantly fell in love with the thrill of speed. He became so engrossed in learning what to do that he told me after he actually felt like an action hero from one of his comic books. Oh, he also became so caught up in the excitement that he almost wet his pants. I remember he shouted, 'Momma! I wanna race cars! Didn't you use to race cars?' And Mother, pleased to pass on her family tradition, said to him, 'Yes, honee. Grandpa Clayton taught me, and now I am showing you.' She repeated a bit of advice that Grandpa Clayton had once told her: 'Sean, honee, I want you to make believe and drive this car as if you just stole it, not like you own it.' Sean just laughed, totally grasping what Mother was trying to tell him." Connor laughed, remembering that he had been told the same thing.

Avery pouted into the phone. "I was so jealous. I was getting a stupid bike for my birthday and Sean got his dream wish. I know this might sound trite, but Sean is my hero for coming out of all this a champion, and so are you, Connor!"

"Thanks, Avery. You should know that to me, you are my hero. Maybe we should all get capes and call ourselves the Mighty Devlins.

Avery laughed and groaned, "*Good-byeeee Connorrrr!*"

*CHAPTER EIGHT*
# *HOTEL ESCONDIDO*

### *ESCAPING TO SOUTH BEACH BEFORE THE RACE*

As soon as they arrived in South Beach, Sean dropped Jimmy off at the hotel curb, and he drove his Sting Ray over to the valet parking attendant. "Hey, Peter, how ya doing?" he said to the attendant, who instantly recognized him.

"Evening, Mr. Sean. You back in town for a visit?" asked Peter.

"Yep, take care of my beauty, oka-a-ay?" Sean teased, holding Peter in a friendly headlock and giving him a few fake punches. Peter always seemed to magically appear whenever Sean visited the hotel, eagerly awaiting the chance to park whichever one of Sean's priceless cars he had arrived in. But Peter knew what Sean really meant behind his joking: *You scratch or ding my car, you're dead.* Peter smiled nervously as Sean tossed him the keys.

Sean caught up with Jimmy at the brightly lit entrance of the Hotel Escondido that jutted out onto the beach. They both breathed in the cool, salty air as they strolled into the lobby which led into a grand atrium, where a huge waterfall was surrounded by exotic rain forest plantings.

Sean smiled and could feel his body become even more alive at the thought he might see Daniella.

They walked to the hotel front desk, smiling and nodding to people who recognized them, and checked in. Sean ate up the attention he got from being PMRA's number-one driver. He even liked the fuss the girls behind the desk made as they giggled and smiled, while Jimmy retreated behind him. Jimmy, whose reputation in the PMRA racing circuit was growing, never liked being in the spotlight and gladly left that for Sean to enjoy. Jimmy was handsome but shy—and totally in the dark about how good looking he was. He was of medium height—wiry but muscular like Sean; he had warm brown eyes with yellow speckles, long and shiny chestnut brown hair, and a cleft in his chin that was a Stanton family characteristic.

Sean recognized the hotel desk manager, a tall, stunning blonde with deep blue eyes. He couldn't remember her name but noticed it on her name tag. "Hi, Rhenea," he said as he snuck another look at her big rack.

"Where's your luggage, boys?" asked Rhenea.

"Ohhh, shoot," said Sean snapping his fingers, slightly red-faced. They had been in such a hurry to get there, he had forgotten to pack any clothes.

Sean smiled at the pretty desk manager. "We like to travel light," he said, winking at her.

"Here are your key cards, gentlemen; I guess you won't need the bellman. But, if you need anything, feel free to check out the shops here at the hotel."

"Yeah," said Sean, "That's a good id..."

Jimmy, totally oblivious to the conversation Sean was having with Rhenea, chimed in, "Avery's waiting for us up in her apartment," breaking Sean's train of thought.

They rode up in the hotel's see-through glass elevator that always made Sean feel like he was going to hurl. No one would ever believe that Sean Devlin—champion race car driver, daredevil, and all-around action junkie—was scared of heights. He could hear his mother's voice in that sweet southern drawl of hers, even after living in New York City for over twenty odd years: '*Sean, honee, never show any weakness, and no stuttering.*'

As they stepped out of the elevator, Sean still felt a little dizzy and nauseous, but shook it off by the time they found Avery's penthouse suite. They pounded on the door and, finding it open, barged in.

The boys were immediately blown away by what Avery had done to her sprawling three thousand square foot hotel apartment since their last visit. Usually Sean was oblivious to designs of any kind, but the new floor-to-ceiling windows with sweeping panoramic views of the waterways made him stop dead in his tracks.

"Wow...Jeez! Jimmy can you believe this view? It's like we're walking on clouds."

They stood there with their mouths hung open. The apartment was sleek and ultramodern. The bare walls were painted in white lacquer. Splashes of black and red accents were thrown in. Several oversized, white, quilted leather and chrome sectional sofas, chaises, and chairs were scattered throughout the gigantic living room. A huge white and black Tibetan wool rug covered most of the living room's white tiled floor. The molded fiberglass red chairs and steel stools looked like they belonged in an art gallery. There were metal sculptures and several of Sean's racing trophies, which Avery was holding for him.

Sean and Jimmy bounded down a long hallway to get to Avery's bedroom. The door was open, so they walked right in and surprised Avery, still in bed with her boyfriend, DJ Sekou. The bed had a navy quilted, leather headboard with a matching leather platform that seemed to be floating amid the bedroom's floor-to-ceiling windows. The walls were stark white with loads of large black and white framed photographs of legendary singers and musicians. The round metal bedside tables and several bookshelves held many picture frames of family and friends.

Avery had the same blue-green eyes, same dimple on the right cheek, and same light build as Sean, except she had all of the right girl parts in the right places. They were both lanky and toned. When people commented on their slender build, Avery would comment in a sarcastic tone, "...And as our mother would say, '*It's best to be throwing-weight thin.*'" Explaining further, she would add, "Our mother was always neurotic about being thin. As far back as I can remember, she had this psycho-irrational fear that if her car crashed or caught fire and she had to be carried or tossed to safety, the thought of her being too heavy for the rescuers was terrifying to her. '*Throwing-weight thin*,' get it? What a loon!"

Sean liked Sekou, a successful rap singer whose real name was Dexter Smith. Avery had met the tall, muscular black man while clubbing with Daniella. Avery told Sean that Sekou's ornate tattoos, hot smile, and very chiseled features made her melt inside. It wasn't long before they hit it off. Sekou was the first decent boyfriend she ever had, and he helped her get off drugs, drinking, and excessive partying. He had been there, done that—Sekou had cleaned up his act for the better and wanted the same for Avery.

Sean leaned over the bed to greet Sekou with a knuckle-to-knuckle fist bump. "Hey, how ya doing Sekou?"

Avery, protesting the intrusion, complained, "Sean, you *idiot*, get the hell outta here! And take your flea-bitten buddy with you."

That stung Jimmy a bit, but he knew she was just kidding. Sean said, "C'mon, you guys. Get up. We drove a long way to see you." Avery and DJ always grabbed a nap around 4:30 p.m., since they had to stay up every night until daybreak.

Avery begged Sean to leave, so she and Sekou could get dressed.

Sean and Jimmy, trying to kill time, wandered out to the living room of the massive suite. Sean looked at some framed pictures on the steel and glass end table. One was of Daniella. The last time they spoke, she wasn't thrilled about his fooling around. She had seen him with other women and broke things off.

Sean stared at the picture. There she was with that awesome red hair—sweet, beautiful Daniella, and what a great body! Right then, Sean wanted to see her *real bad*!

Sean was trying so hard to hide his interest in seeing her, but Avery, now dressed, came into the living room and saw him holding Daniella's picture and blurted out, "So, you miss her, dear bro of mine?" Sean turned to look at Avery, sporting that devilish grin, and fumbled to put the picture back in its place on the table. Avery greeted each of the boys warmly with a hug and a kiss. She always read Se-

41

an's mind and made him blush. He knew he was about to be brutally teased about Daniella.

"Oh, um, how is she, by the way?" Sean asked sheepishly.

"Well, she's fine, and you?"

Sean clenched his teeth, not letting his sister get the better of him. "I'm not playin', Avery..."

"You should have seen the dude she was with last night."

Then Jimmy piped up and said, "You should have seen the girl Sean was with last night—I mean, this morning."

"Blah blah blah," said Sekou as he entered the living room "Hey guys, you're out of high school now; enough with the game playing! Honestly!"

They all laughed at Sekou's uncharacteristic choice of words. Avery walked over to the wet bar and began pulling out mixers. "Hey guys, how about a drink?"

Sean grinned and said, "Thought you'd never ask!"

She held up a bottle of rye. "Manhattans all around?"

Sean joked, "Don't you have any of that wine in a box?"

Avery made a frown of disapproval.

Jimmy smiled at Avery and said, "I never had one of your Manhattans before, Avery."

Sekou walked over to the large entertainment center and put on his new CD. He said, "Hey, guys, I wanna play you my latest jam."

Avery offered drinks to everybody and gushed, "Yeah, I really like this mix he put together. Wait 'til you hear it!"

She sat down near Jimmy and they all got comfortable. Jimmy closed his eyes, taking in Avery's familiar tea rose scent. The music was an exciting blend of hip-hop and rap that had a catchy sound with amazing lyrics. Avery got up and started to dance by herself. Jimmy bobbed his head to the beat of the music and then jumped up to join her. He grabbed her and started to draw her close, but she darted away toward Sekou. Sean was tapping his feet and missed the whole thing.

The music ended, and everyone clapped for Sekou.

"Great stuff, man," said Sean.

"Yeah! That was all right!" echoed Jimmy.

"They're all going to go crazy at the clubs for your new mix. It's awesome!" said Sean.

"Cool, thanks a lot," said Sekou. "I'm gonna try it out tonight."

"C'mon, guys," Avery said as she put her cocktail glass down. "Since you're in South Beach and on my turf, let me show you a good time!"

Jimmy was always looking for some action, so he asked Avery if there were any card games going on. "Yeah, Jimmy," she said. "I'll call my friend Aubrey and find you one. What I really wanted to say was, tonight I'm throwing a special party for you both at Club Sucre, a good luck before the race *par-tee*. So Jimmy, don't get lost the way you usually do." She stood up and started to clean. "Oh shoot, guys! I just remembered you're gonna have to grab dinner by yourselves tonight. Sekou and I have to get going to the club to make the final arrangements for your party."

"Oh...okay. Thanks, that's great, guys!" said Sean. "We'll see you later then at the club."

Sean and Jimmy decided to eat at a popular local sport's bar, Buzzy's. It was always crowded, but the boys reserved a table all the way in the back where they wouldn't be noticed. They hated to be hassled for autographs while they were eating. The bar had several large screen TVs with the latest sports and the food was really good.

**AVERY AND DJ** headed out to Club Sucre. Sekou was anxious to work on the new mix in his overhead sound booth for the boys' party.

As they were walking to their car, Sekou turned to Avery and said, "So what's up with you two? You and Jimmy, I mean. I noticed he was crowdin' your style when you were dancing. He's crushin' on you, huh?"

"Oh yeah, but I've never encouraged him. It goes all the way back to when we were kids. It's always been one-sided. I've always treated him like a brother all these years. I go easy on him because he had a crappy childhood."

"So what's his story?" asked Sekou. "I'm curious. I've always liked Jimmy."

"Well, Sean and I spent a lot of time with Jimmy when we were growing up, and Jimmy was treated just like another member of our family. He and Sean were best buddies from the time they were ten years old; they met at that hellhole Trent Military Academy for Boys."

"Military academy? Say wha?"

"Yeah. It's a boarding school up in New Haven, Connecticut. My mother thought it would do Sean some good and straighten his ass out. Jimmy was there for a different reason. Jimmy had had a mother who was a beautiful, southern socialite. Anyway, she up and walked out on Jimmy's father when Jimmy was only three years old."

"Jeez, that's tough," said Sekou. "A kid that young...losing his momma? Damn! So what about his old man?"

Avery continued, "His father is William Stanton III, a very prominent attorney in Atlanta. He told Jimmy his mother was very sick and had to go to a hospital up north. There were rumors that Emily had run off to follow her dream of singing, but no one ever found out what really happened to her. His father hired several detectives to find her, but they never did. Jimmy and his father never heard from her again."

Sekou looked at Avery and said, "When people don't want to be found, they usually aren't. Something must have happened to her."

Avery frowned and said, "What do you mean?"

Sekou reconsidered what he was going to say. "I don't know, baby. I'm just sayin'." He tried to distract her back to the story she was telling. "Hey, why do they call him JP? Those aren't his initials."

Avery answered, "Jimmy got his nickname from the local kids when he was in his early teens. To beat his boredom, he would hot-wire police cars and go joyriding all over Atlanta without being caught. He soon became a legend—Jimmy the Policeman, or JP."

Sekou rubbed the back of his neck in amazement. "Legend? Shit, if he was black, they would have *legended* his ass to jail."

"They almost did, babe. Fortunately, his father had a few friends on the force. Jimmy's dad did the best he could to raise Jimmy right, but by the time Jimmy was into his teens, he was too wild and rebellious. So his father would call some of the local cops he knew to try and teach Jimmy a lesson. Knowing Mr. Stanton's dilemma, the local police showed a bit more compassion for Jimmy and tried to go easy on him. There was some cop there, what was his name? Oh yeah, Ray Barber. He kept an eye on Jimmy and found out that he loved to fix cars and especially liked going to the races on weekends. This Officer Barber guy recognized Jimmy's natural ability as a race car driver and knew that all this kid needed was someone to recognize a hurting soul and rescue him—kinda like puttin' lightnin' in a bottle. Ray Barber talked Jimmy into enrolling in the Peachtree Auto Racing Academy where Ray taught in his off hours. Jimmy began spending a lot of time hanging around Ray and attending his classes. So JP became a permanent nickname, and racing cars became his life."

"Wow!" said Sekou. "And I thought I had it tough as a kid. Lightnin' in a bottle...That's about right! He always seems like he is going to explode at any second. Now I know why you've treated him with kid gloves, babe."

## CHAPTER NINE
# *GETTING READY TO PARTY*

A fter dinner, Sean got a call from Marco Reinaldo, owner of Leroux, the exclusive men's boutique in the Hotel Escondido, letting him know that their party clothes were ready and waiting for them in his shop. He and Marco had spoken earlier about what suits the boys wanted to wear to Avery's party. Sean's Hugo Boss suit was in black with a white silk T-shirt under his jacket, and JP's was in silver gray, also with a white silk T-shirt.

Sean thanked Marco. "Great job! I don't know how you pulled it all together so quickly. I'm sure you'll see our pictures in the papers tomorrow wearing your clothes."

"Boys, I'm only too happy to help. I'll have it all delivered to your rooms at once. "Have a good time tonight and good-luck with the races. See you next time," Marco said.

**HITTING THE GYM** and working out was next.

"Nah!" said Jimmy. "I've changed my mind. I'd rather go find a card game."

*Oh crap!* thought Sean. "Hey JP!" he said, "Don't get your ass in a jam! Damn! If I have to bail your effing butt out of trouble one more time, I will *personally*…just know you'll have pain in parts of your body you never knew existed!"

"Okay, okay," said Jimmy. "I'll play later. Maybe I'll go running on that outside track and then go for a swim. I promise." Jimmy was always like a man-child, but he was a great buddy.

Just as he was about to dive into the hotel's indoor Olympic-sized pool, Sean heard his cell phone ring. He went to grab it out of one of his new Crocs sandals. It was his friend Hank in Ormond Beach.

Sean and Hank Cho became fast friends when Sean's brother, Connor, married Hank's sister, Genji. Hank, twenty-six years old, an engineer at DMS, quickly rose up in the ranks becoming indispensable to Ace and Connor. When Hank wasn't occupied with DMS business, he would hang out with Sean. Hank, very detail oriented, and highly organized, began to take over the reins of Sean's life when he caught on quickly that his good friend was hopeless in dealing with the day-to-day things.

"How ya doing, Hank, my good man?"

Hank responded in his usual rapid-fire speech: "Fine! Sean, you forgot to feed Slate! Where are you? Your dad, Connor, and everyone will be arriving in Ormond Beach at twenty-one hours tomorrow. Slate has a girlfriend, and dammit Sean, you forgot to buy dog food. I did your laundry, and did you party last night? Anyway where are you?…*Where*? Are you *nuts*? Aren't you supposed to be practicing for Sunday's race? What about the Gator next week? And what clothes did you take? Did you even pack? All your stuff is still here!"

After that earful, Sean tried to appease Hank, saying, "Yeah, yeah, no, and yeah. Hank, what would I do without you?"

Hank was making faces at his phone on the other end and making gagging noises back at Sean.

"Hey Hank, Jimmy and I are hangin' with Avery and Sekou. We'll be coming back home tomorrow…not too late…I promise. Oh, by the way, thanks for taking care of Slate and everything else. So, Slate has a girlfriend? Hmmm." Sean, noticing a very pretty girl dive into the pool, said, "Gotta go play lifeguard now! Thanks, Hank." Hank closed his cell and said out loud, "Did he say *lifeguard*? What the…"

## CHAPTER TEN
# ECSTASY AND AGONY

L ater that night things started to come alive. There was an unusually warm tropical breeze for February, putting everybody in a festive mood. The boys entered Club Sucre, greeting the bouncer with warm high-fives and handshakes.

Avery had tastefully redecorated the club in the sleek art deco design. The walls were mauve and gray. There were the distinctive deco crystal and chrome wall lights, as well as hundreds of spotlights in the vaulted ceiling. There were many neon lit bars all over the club. They gave the illusion of being magically suspended with frosted glass bar stools. Hundreds of people sat comfortably in the plush mauve, velvet banquettes spread all over the club, and VIP's hid in the private back rooms, doing their own thing out of view of the press. The three thousand square foot dance floor was in off-white marble so everyone could see where they were dancing and watch everyone else. High above, the club had several wraparound balconies where people could look down at the crowds.

As Sean and Jimmy entered the club, their senses were immediately on overload with the glaring jewels of light showering over thousands of people from all over the globe. Sean recognized some faces, but there were a lot more he didn't know at first without prompting. He always got a kick out of his sister's ability to pick people out of a crowd and identify them, even from the back of their heads. But at the moment, he couldn't find Avery. "What a mob! Jimmy, do you see Avery anywhere?"

There were loads of people dancing to the hip-hop music that DJ Sekou spun from his glass booth high atop the dance floor, their bending bodies melting rhythmically into their dancing partners as if they were making love. Jimmy spotted Avery way across the crowded floor. "There she is! Follow me, Sean."

"Oh yeah, I see her now," Sean said, looking over Jimmy's shoulder.

After wading through the throngs, they finally caught up to her. She looked very pretty in her shocking green and turquoise sequined halter top. As they came up behind her, Jimmy said, "Hey, Avery! You look awesome!"

Avery turned her head to see Jimmy and Sean grinning at her. "Hi, guys!" Her smile revealed her delight. "You made it!" She shouted to her immediate circle of party friends, "Hey! They're here! Say hello to my brother, Sean, and my good friend, Jimmy Stanton."

Everybody greeted the boys and shook their hands. An attractive waitress brought over a tray full of Long Island iced teas and offered the boys a drink. They were momentarily distracted by her short skirt and watched her walk away. Avery caught them staring and laughed, "Guys, over here?"

"Aw, Sis, you have outdone yourself. This is awesome. Where did you find..."

Suddenly, Sean stopped talking midsentence. Avery saw her brother's eyes land on a beautiful, familiar figure. "Ahhh," she said, kissing Sean and leaning over to say, "Go get-tah, dear brother."

Sean said, "I have to give it to you, Sis. You sure know how to throw a great party." He kissed his sister back and said, "See you later!"

Avery took Jimmy aside, despite a gnawing feeling that told her that she was going to regret it. She said, "I'll set up a card game for you, but *please* behave. And you bet-tah come back to your room tonight or we will, including Sean, be *killed* by my whole family. Got that?"

Dodging Avery's wagging finger, Jimmy nodded yes and suddenly drifted over to a good looking girl; he gave his special signal to Sean that he was going to take a detour for a while, and then vaporized into the vortex of dancers.

Sean's heart began to pound so rapidly, he felt like he was going to pass out. *This is ridiculous. I'm a grown man*, he thought. Suddenly the mad crush of people and all the noise faded into thin air, and all he could see was the beautiful redhead across the room. He needed fresh air. Not even the Gator 500 could make him this nervous. But... oh no, she started walking through the crowds until she stood right in front of him. He stammered, "D-D-D-Daniella." Damn it! Every time he thought his childhood stutter was gone for good, certain people would make it return.

"Hiya, stranger," she said in her smooth and crisp voice. She promised herself and Avery she wasn't going to fall all over him, since he was the one that messed up their relationship. But once she saw him, all of her resolve melted away, and she took his hand and they went out back to sit on the patio. The music was playing outside, but he could hardly hear it.

Daniella whispered in his ear, "Miss me? Avery told me you were coming for a visit."

His body ached for her, and he showed her how much he missed her by grabbing her close and kissing her long and hard. At first, she resisted, but the ice quickly melted. She pulled him closer and opened her mouth for a fuller kiss. She wanted to remind him just what he had been missing with all his foolishness with other women. Message received. He felt like he was safe again, and he vowed to himself that he would never let her get away again. Sean looked into her eyes, and a million thoughts rushed through his brain. He tried hard to hold back his tears, not wanting to betray his true feelings. The voice in his head said, *Do something, stupid!*

He took her hand and said, "C'mon, Red! Let's go for a ride."

"But Sean, what about your party? Avery would never forgive you if you left."

He looked around at all the unfamiliar faces, drinking and smiling and dancing, and he said, "Babe, these people would never miss me! Besides, Avery will be happy to know we are getting reacquainted."

She looked deeply into his eyes, smiling brightly, and they went to get his car.

Sean drove to a secluded spot on the beach where they talked quietly while listening to the breaking surf. Sean really wanted to patch things up with Daniella. They kissed tenderly, and she finally forgave him. Then, the rekindled fire in their hearts consumed the two lovers, and they kissed more passionately. A Corvette was no place to accommodate their needs. Sean fired up the car and took off for the hotel.

Sean and Daniella burst through the door of his hotel room, kissing and embracing, tearing at their clothes as if they were on fire. In that moment, they needed each other desperately. The two were lost in passion, seeking to become one. His body pulsed rhythmically every few seconds as they cried out together with ecstasy. They clung to each other and made love over and over, making up for the lost time apart, climaxing more outrageously each time before crescendoing into an explosion of such magnitude that they collapsed and fell off to sleep in sated exhaustion. In that moment, Sean realized how much he loved her. *Nothing will come between us again*, he thought to himself.

*Bam! Bam! Bam!* "Wh-what the..." *Bam! Bam! Bam!* Sean awoke to a loud, desperate pounding at the door; he heard Jimmy's muffled cries for help: "Sean! Sean, let me in! They're after me, Sean! Open up the door!"

He jumped out of bed and pulled on his shorts, trying not to wake up Daniella. In a hazy state, he ran to open the door. All of a sudden, some wild looking thugs shoved Jimmy through the doorway, jumped on Sean, and tasered him on the right side of his head. He fell to the floor and lay there, deadly still, as if he were paralyzed. Somehow he was able to squint and peer through one eye and see them chloroform Jimmy and then cover his head with a large bag. As they dragged him out the door, one of them yelled, "That's for the five hundred grand he owes us."

Daniella was jarred awake from a deep sleep when she heard a door slam. *Was that someone moaning?* she thought and instinctively reached over to feel for Sean's warm body. After finding his side of the bed empty, she called out, "Sean? Sean, where are you?" She heard moaning again, so she pulled a sheet around her naked body and hurried into the next room where she almost tripped over his body. Sean was lying immobile and still on the hotel room floor. Alarmed, she shrieked, "Oh my God! Sean, what happened? Sean, speak to me!"

Sean could barely open his eyes; the room was spinning. *Damn JP*, he thought. His mouth felt like cotton candy, and he tried very hard to form the words to tell Daniella what had happened.

She raced over to the hotel phone. "Hello, hello, Geraldo? Please have the doctor come to Mr. Devlin's room immediately. It's an emergency, but please do not tell Avery or anyone else. Do you understand me, Geraldo? Thank you!" She slammed the receiver back into the cradle and rushed back to her lover. "Sean, talk to me....Keep talking to me." She dashed back to the bedroom and quickly got dressed before the doctor arrived.

Daniella knew she had to keep Sean awake in case the taser had caused a serious head injury. She ran over to the ice bucket and filled a towel with cubes, putting it on the side of Sean's head where the taser had caused a deep laceration.

"Ow! Ow! Oww!" yelled Sean. "That hurts!" He could barely move no matter how much he tried. "That damn taser," he cried aloud.

There was another banging on the door. *Thank God*, Daniella thought when she looked through the peephole and saw Dr. Tomas Rivera, fortyish, and highly professional, who was well acquainted with the Devlin family and could always be relied upon on for his discretion and trust. "

"Okay, Sean and Daniella, what happened?"

Sean curled into a fetal position and blurted out, obviously in pain, "Uhn! I was attacked. I don't remember what happened. It all happened so fast, but I think somebody kidnapped Jimmy. I think som..." His voice trailed off as he desperately grasped at his fractured bits of memory.

The doctor examined him and said, "It looks like you have burns and a nasty laceration on the side of your head. Hmmm. Look Sean, I should really take you to the hospital for a full evaluation."

"Doc, I can't have anyone finding out about this yet. Just patch me up as best as you can."

Dr. Rivera gave Sean a local anesthetic and sutured the wound. "Keep him quiet and I'll check on him in a few hours," said Dr. Rivera. "Now Sean, I know you have two big races coming up, so can you please try to take it easy? I'll prescribe painkillers for you, but I don't want you to overuse them, especially since, no doubt, you'll want to drive out of here the minute I leave. You need to take care of yourself. These pills *will* make you drowsy." Dr. Rivera scribbled on his prescription pad. "I'll have the hotel pharmacy send them up to your room right away."

"Screw the pills, Doc! Owww!"

"Sean, you really must pay attention to me. Daniella, make sure he follows my orders." He told Sean, "Go to your doctor in Ormond Beach if you have any complications. Okay? Or you can call me if you feel like you're not getting any better."

Sean and Daniella thanked Dr. Rivera as he left. The minute the doctor was gone, Sean attempted to stand up but couldn't. Parts of his body were still numb. His head ached, and he was still feeling woozy. Daniella scolded him and said, "Sean honey, rest for a bit, and then I'll drive you back to Ormond Beach. You're in no shape to drive."

Sean responded curtly, "No, no, I'm fine."

Daniella took a firmer stance. "No, you're *not* fine. You need to rest. The doctor warned you! You won't be any good for the race tomorrow if you don't take care of yourself."

"Okay, okay...I hear ya," said Sean as he leaned back and put his hand to his aching head. "We gotta do something to find Jimmy."

"I think you should speak to your father," said Daniella.

"Oh crap!" said Sean. "That's all I need—to get reamed out by my father. So much for having fun in South Beach. I can already hear him."

"Sean! You should be thinking about Jimmy, not yourself."

"You're right. Let me have the phone." Sean leaned forward. "Oooh! Maybe I better take it easy a little longer."

Daniella held the phone and said, "Do you want me to call him for you...or maybe we should phone the police?"

"No cops! Not before we talk to Dad. Gimme the phone."

Sean thought out loud, "Damn it, Jimmy! Why couldn't you have stayed out of trouble?"

Sean listened to the phone. "Crap, it's the voicemail. I should have known better; it's five in the morning. I can't leave a message like this on his voicemail!"

Daniella took the phone and hung it up, saying, "We'll call him later when we drive back to Ormond Beach."

Thinking more clearly, they both agreed that something wasn't quite right about how Jimmy had been kidnapped.

"You know, Red, those guys that took Jimmy did look familiar. But I can't remember where I saw them before."

Sean would have to wait a few more hours to call his father. He said to Daniella, "I'll let my dad handle the police and the press. Holy crap! If word got out about what happened down here, all hell would break loose and really mess things up for Jimmy and DMS! So it's better to keep it under wraps. Dad will know what to do. He always does. Jeez, I better call my sister next." He pulled out his cell phone and called Avery. "Sis, it's me. Sorry I'm waking you."

"Sean? No, you're not waking us. We just got back from the club. Say, where'd you disappear to?"

"Avery, please listen to me!"

"Hey, what's wrong, bro?"

Sean blurted out, "Jimmy was jumped and kidnapped a few hours ago...right in front of me...in my hotel room. I heard pounding on my door and when I opened it, there was Jimmy yelling for help. A couple of goons zapped me in the head with a taser, chloroformed Jimmy, and dragged him off. They yelled something about Jimmy owing them five hundred thousand dollars."

"No... Can't be!" she shouted into the phone, blasting his eardrum and freaking out Sekou. "I told that bugger how much trouble we would be in if he messed up. He swore to me he wouldn't do anything *stupid*." Avery began to cry.

"Avery. Avery, listen to me....Listen! It's water under the bridge now, so snap out of it." Sean tried a more compassionate approach. "Sis, please stop crying. We have to act fast and smart; you should stay here with Sekou. I'm going to call Dad. Wait until Dad gets back to you. Keep quiet and don't call the cops. Yes, I'm going to call D-D-Dad next. He's supposed to come down from New York with Connor and Genji tomorrow. Dad always knows how to handle these things."

"Sean, I'm so afraid for Jimmy," she sobbed. "I feel so responsible."

"Stay cool, Sis. W-w-we'll find out what's going on."

"Oh, Sean," she whispered, "I'm scared."

"I know, Av. Not to worry—your bro will find JP, and ya know I love ya, Sis. I'll always take care of you."

"Yeah, I know you do. Okay, Sean, I love ya back."

After hanging up from his heavy conversation with Avery, Sean, lost in thought, began tossing his stuff into the new luggage he and JP had bought. He'd have to have Avery pack up Jimmy's stuff. He said to Daniella, "Look, Red, I really don't have time to wait for you to pack. Maybe it would be better if you stayed behind with Avery. After I talk to my d-dad, we can figure out what to do next, but right now I gotta get out of here!"

"It's okay, Sean," said Daniella. "You'll make better time without me. Just let me know what is going on, and please take it slow, okay honey?"

Daniella called down to the front desk and said, "Hello? Oh Geraldo, good, you're still on duty. Yes, please have someone drive Mr. Devlin's car over to the front of the hotel. Thank you, Geraldo...we'll be right down."

Daniella held onto Sean very tightly; he wrapped one of his arms around her neck and they slowly made it to the elevator. They walked slowly through the lobby to the glass front doors. Sean's car was out front. The valet rushed over to assist Sean. Daniella and the valet carefully guided Sean over to the driver's side, and he slowly slid into the car.

They kissed goodbye tenderly, and he tried to hold it together as he watched Daniella walk back into the hotel. Suddenly, the cold hard reality of Jimmy's kidnapping kicked in, and Sean became even more frightened. As for Jimmy, why wasn't Sean surprised that wherever Jimmy went, trouble always followed? He hoped he could keep that promise to Avery.

## CHAPTER ELEVEN
# WHERE'S JIMMY?

### A DAY BEFORE THE RACE

Jimmy woke up in a fog. He was lying on a cold concrete floor, tied up in a room that looked like a bunker. Confused, he didn't know how he got there. The last thing Jimmy remembered, was being at a card game that Avery's friend Aubrey had arranged for him. The game was in a room off Club Bezo's main floor. There were some rough looking guys that Jimmy had never seen before. After he played a few hands of poker, he was offered a drink by one of them. Things got hazy after that. He played a few more hands of cards and began to lose heavily. Jimmy realized the game was fixed and in a panic he fled. Staggering out, he began pushing people out of his way, as he frantically tried to get to the main entrance to escape. The big burly thugs were hot on his heels, but had a tougher time getting through the crowds. Once outside, Jimmy hailed the first cab he saw and sped away. Whatever they had put in his drink had made him feel very sick and weak. He had to get back to Sean at the hotel. He didn't realize the men chasing him had followed him up to Sean's room. As they forced their way through the door, they overtook the boys. One of the thugs shouted out that Stanton owed them five hundred grand. The boys struggled with them and one guy subdued and tasered Sean while the other man held Jimmy down and chloroformed him. That was the last thing Jimmy remembered.

Jimmy didn't know how long he had been out. His head began to pound and he felt very nauseous. He tried to take a mental snapshot of his surroundings. The walls looked like they were fifteen feet high. Everything was painted battleship gray. He was going in and out of consciousness. Jimmy freaked out when he saw the name 'Clayton' in red paint on one of the walls. He had heard that Clayton had a warehouse a few miles outside of Ormond Beach.

He tried to read what was on a big computer screen that showed confidential technical data on all of their racing cars and their competitors, but his eyes couldn't focus and things looked blurry. Jimmy had seen similar computers that the Devlin racing team used, but clearly not as advanced.

Full of drugs, he nodded off. He was abruptly awakened by someone who sounded like Benecio Villereal. He was nudged again, and he slowly opened his eyes and blinked. He couldn't tell if it was day or night. "Yeah, he's still breathing," the person said.

A feeling of dread overtook him, and he kept mumbling out loud over and over, "Where's Sean? Sean..." Jimmy blacked out again.

## CHAPTER TWELVE

# A RACE AGAINST TIME

## SATURDAY: THE DAY BEFORE THE TRIAX 400 RACE

After leaving the hotel en route to Ormond Beach, Sean had to pull over. He felt too groggy from his pain medicine to drive any further. He said to himself, "Daniella was right. I needed more rest before taking this trip." His head wound from the taser assault the night before, was still throbbing with intense pain. Sean decided to kill time at a nearby DK Donut Shop. He thought, *I have to be clear headed when I tell my dad about what happened to Jimmy.* He had a few cups of DK's great coffee and by the time he got back into his car in the parking lot, he dozed off.

Two hours later, the coffee in his system jolted him awake. He opened his eyes and glanced at his cell phone which read 8:15 in the morning. "Now or never," he said to himself. His hand trembled as he punched in his father's cell phone number. Ace answered immediately. "Hey, son. What's up?"

"D-Dad?" Sean said. "We got trouble—*big time!*"

Ace called out to his assistant, Monica, to come into his office. Sean said, "Dad, were you just talking to Monica? What are you doing at the office so early?"

"I wanted to get caught up before flying down tonight for tomorrow's race. Now, what's the trouble?"

Sean blurted out, "Dad, th-they kidnapped Jimmy! W-what are we gonna do?"

All that emotion Sean was holding in check suddenly rushed to the surface.

"Christ *Almighty*!" Ace walked over to his office bar and poured himself a bourbon despite the early hour. "Okay, son, tell me everything."

"JP and I were visiting Avery in South Beach f-for the night. Something happened. A couple of big g-guys b-broke into my hotel room and attacked us. They tasered me and then kidnapped JP over a gambling debt." Sean took a deep breath to relieve the tension building in his body. "They said he owed f-five hundred grand."

"What?" yelled Ace. His father rarely raised his voice, so Sean knew he was *really* pissed. Ace yelled, "You knew you and JP had to get your arses in geah for the Triax 400 tomorrow and the Gator 500 next Saturday. What the hell were you thinking going AWOL like that? Damn it all, Sean! And furthermore, why the *hell* did you let JP go and *gamble*? You know he has a problem. I really don't want to know how Jimmy got involved with a bunch of hustlers. God almighty!" Ace gulped down his drink, and swallowed hard. "Okay, son, start over again. Exactly what happened?"

Sean retold the story as best as he could recall (but left out all of the hot details about getting back together with Daniella). Finally, Sean asked, "S-so when can you and Connor get down here?"

Ace sat at his desk, fuming. His employees at DMS were under attack. He knew that this was directly related to the upcoming races. There was always friendly competition between racing garages, but this kidnapping showed that someone wanted to weaken the Devlin Motor Sports racing team by sabotaging their drivers. "D-Dad? You still there?" Sean startled his father back to the phone conversation.

"Sean, I want you to get out of wherever you are and go hide out in the DMS RV. Now! *Do you heah me?* Go now!"

"B-but D-Dad, I'm still in South Beach. I'll be driving back to Ormond Beach as soon as I get off the phone with you. I was g-going to call Billy Ray to have him look for Jimmy with me."

"Now, son, don't go off half-cocked."

Ace was already putting together a list of suspects in his head.

"We have to think this through. I'll call Billy Ray and tell him to go pick up your mother at our Ormond Beach condo and meet up with you at the company's RV at the track."

"Are you sure, D-Dad? I mean, I c-cou..."

"You just listen to me, Sean. Now that I think about it, when you get back, have Dakota meet you at your place and then you both go to the team's RV."

"What about D-Daniella, Dad? What should we do about Daniella, Avery, and Sekou?"

"I'll make arrangements for them to fly to Ormond Beach tonight too and meet up with all of us. We'll all be together for tomorrow's race.

"But D-Dad, maybe I should get D-Daniella..."

"Just listen to me, son! I'll handle everything from heah!" I'll have my security guy in Miami look after them and follow-up on any leads for Jimmy. Don't worry, son. They'll be all right."

"Okay, okay, good. C-call me when you have something, Dad!"

"Yes, and keep in touch. Call me from the road so I know you are all right, Sean. Try not to draw attention to yourself."

"Okay, D-Dad. Later!"

Ace hung up the phone and looked at Monica with a grave expression; his hand trembled as he held his drink. "Monica," he said, "something has come up, and I need you to stay late. Can you?"

Monica nodded and said, "Of course. What's happened, Mr. Devlin?"

"I'm not completely sure, but if my hunch is right, somebody is trying to sabotage our racing business, by harming our drivers."

The young executive assistant was alarmed. "Sabotage! Shouldn't we call the police?"

"No, this is something I have to handle myself. If I'm right, involving the law would just muck up everything."

"What do you want me to do?"

"Hmm...For now, I want you to get Avery on the phone. ...And Monica?"

"Yes, sir?"

"I'm going to need your complete discretion heah."

"If your family is in trouble, I'll do whatever it takes to help."

"Thank you, deah."

Ace managed a weak smile, and Monica smiled back before retreating to her desk. A minute later, the intercom buzzed and she said, "Mr. Devlin, I have Avery on the phone."

"Thanks."

"Oh, Daddy, I've been waiting to hear from you. Sean said you'd be calling me." Avery was in tears.

"Honey, why the hell did you get Jimmy involved in a card game? What the hell were you thinking?"

"Daddy, I swear it was supposed to be a friendly game. I trusted my friend, Aubrey, but somehow these creeps conned their way into the game, flashing around a lot of money. I warned Jimmy he betta not get in trouble. I even told him that you'd kill us if he didn't come back from the game early. Dad, I really thou..."

"Avery, you're a smaht girl; don't you know that a leopard nevah changes his spots?"

"Oh, Daddy, not the leopard lecture again."

"And involving your brother? Now honey, I need to get in touch with your friend Aubrey. Who is he and what's his numbah?"

"Well, Dad, I've known him for a long time, and he's never let me down. He works at the hotel as a concierge and always knows how to make things happen. He's my go-to guy."

"Have you called him lately to see if he heard anything new or had any fresh ideahs about what might have happened to Jimmy?"

"Yeah, I called him, but he didn't have much to say."

Ace remembered his daughter's past struggles and tried to tone down his anger and talk to her more sweetly.

"Deah, tell me how to get in touch with him."

"Daddy, you're not going to hurt him, are you?"

"No, Avery, we just want to find Jimmy."

She gave her father Aubrey's phone number.

"Now I want you to get your people at work to cover for you, Sekou, and Daniella for today and tomorrow. I'll arrange to have a plane pick you all up and take you to Ormond Beach tonight. Can you do that?"

"Okay, Daddy."

"I also want to remind you your brother is racing in the Triax 400 tomorrow afternoon."

Ace then lowered his voice, so Monica wouldn't hear him get mushy with his only baby girl. "Honey, you know Daddy loves you; I'm going to do everything possible to get Jimmy back and find out what's going on."

"Thanks, Daddy. I love you, too," she said, tearing up. "One more thing," she said. "How's Sean feeling?"

"You know your brother has a hard head, so don't you worry! Gotta go now. Will get back to you with fuhtha instructions."

He hung up the phone, hoping he wasn't too hard on his daughter. He shouted out, "Monica, get me Rick Gardner in Miami on the phone. Then I want you to track down Connah. He's needs to know about this."

**SEAN DROVE ON** autopilot and somehow arrived back at his Ormond Beach RV in one piece. Still weak from his taser ordeal and drained by Jimmy's kidnapping, he walked into his RV and tossed the bottle of pain pills that Dr. Rivera had given him on the table. Slate ran in barking like crazy when he saw Sean. He jumped up, almost toppling him over. Sean was so ecstatic to see him. He gave the dog several hugs and scratched him behind the ears.

Hank, hearing all the commotion, came running to see what was going on. He gasped after seeing Sean's bandaged head. "What happened to you? Why are you back so soon? What's going on, Sean?" Oh my God, Will you be able to race tomorrow?"

Sean explained what happened to him and Jimmy back in South Beach, and that his father was taking security measures to protect DMS from more trouble. Sean told Hank that Ace wanted Dakota to drive here, so then they would both travel together to the company RV. Hank, still reeling from the news, and seeing what bad shape Sean was in, persuaded him to take his pain medication and go to bed.

It was a good thing Ace had given Hank a list of things to do before he found out about the terrible things that happened. Otherwise, Hank would have totally panicked. He went to gas up Sean's SUV. He reviewed his checklist while multitasking—securing everything in Sean's RV and taking his own iPad with Ace's confidential DMS data. Hank thought, *I'll wait until Sean wakes up and then I'll leave.* He shouted to Sean's dog, "Slate! Where are you, boy? Come on, Slate, do your business now."

**ACE'S NEXT CALL** was to Billy Ray. Ace could depend on Billy Ray to follow orders in a crisis. Ace brought him up to speed on Sean's attack and Jimmy's disappearance. He told Billy Ray to discreetly explain to their other crew chiefs the breach in security and sabotage problems DMS was having. Ace said, "Tell them to keep a sharp eye out for trouble; otherwise, maintain business as usual. "

Ace told Billy Ray to go pick up Taylor at the condo, saying, "Keep your company two-way cell phone on, Billy, and do not tell anybody else what is going down. No cops! We will all meet at the DMS RV at the track. Go in the side door."

Billy Ray grasped the gravity of the situation. "Okay, boss. Consider it done. Ace, what about Dakota?"

"Don't worry Billy. I'm going to have her meet Sean at his place, and then he'll drive her to the company RV."

Billy Ray thought Ace's plan made sense and agreed that it would be a good idea to keep their racing crews in the dark about what had happened to the boys so as not to distract them from their work. Billy

Ray told his crew and the others that he had just gotten off the phone with Ace, and Ace wanted them to recheck all points on each race car. With that, the crews all started to work on all the DMS cars which would keep them busy for the whole day and night.

**SEAN WOKE UP** from his nap and felt like his head was stuffed with cotton. He was disoriented, and for a minute, he forgot he was back in his RV in Ormond Beach. His taser wound still hurt like hell. Hank heard him stirring and came running in with Slate. Slate jumped all over Sean and licked his face.

"Hey, Sean," said Hank. "Remember you have to call Dakota and tell her to meet you here. I have to leave now. I'll see you later."

Hank saw Sean fumbling around trying to get himself together and said, "Sean, you have too much to do. Let me take Slate now. C'mon Slate! You're with me."

Sean hugged his dog and spoke to him, "Get going, boy, I'll see you soon.

Hank said, "Later, Bud!" Sean nodded with a smile.

He heard Hank's SUV drive off.

Sean splashed cold water on his face. He called Dakota and told her what was going on and what Ace wanted her to do.

She responded, "Look Sean, I don't feel very well, and I'm kind of tired. You go on ahead without me, and I'll meet you all there later, okay? Thanks for calling. Bye."

He shrugged it off knowing how independent she was, and continued to get ready. Sean smiled as he thought back to when he first saw Dakota.

It was about eight years ago, when Dakota and Billy Ray were hired by Ace for Devlin Motorsports. They had just graduated from PMRA's Driver and Mechanic Training School in North Carolina. Sean happened to be there when Ace was introducing them to the team and crew. Sean was still in training and hadn't begun racing formally for

DMS. Dakota was drop-dead gorgeous and Sean developed a crush on her and was still infatuated with her to this day. She was Billy Ray's girl and was all about the business of racing. She never was interested in Sean, but he could always dream.

Refocusing on what he was doing, Sean jammed his stuff in a bag in preparation for tomorrow's race. It was eating him up inside that Jimmy was still missing, but Sean had to keep pushing ahead so he'd be psyched up to win the race. He was about to grab his gear and walk out when his cell phone rang. It was his dad.

Sean grabbed his phone and said, "Hi D-Dad! ...Oh g-good, both jets have landed. ...Yeah I'm f-feeling okay... I was just leaving... No, D-Dakota told me she wasn't feeling well, but that she'd meet everyone there later... Dad, could you please tell D-Daniella I'll see her there soon, and say 'Hi' to the f-family for me... Yeah, I'm on m-my way now... Thanks... Love you too, Dad."

## CHAPTER THIRTEEN
# REALITY CHECK

### SEAN'S RECOVERY RIGHT AFTER TRIAX

S ean's nightmares had foretold of his fiery fatal crash at the Triax race. His nightmares almost came true, but miraculously, Sean survived the crash and only ended up with a knee injury and a concussion.

Sean had to have emergency surgery to repair a torn lateral meniscus in his left knee. He had been recuperating in the hospital for several days.

It was late afternoon when Sean got a call from Billy Ray letting him know that he was bringing Sean's mother to pick him up at the hospital the next morning when Sean was being discharged. They had been in touch every day.

Sean could tell that something was troubling Billy Ray, and he wanted to be supportive of him. They had always looked out for each other like brothers. Sean guessed it had something to do with Dakota, since she wasn't acting like herself lately.

"Hey, Billy," he said. "Anything new? How ya doing?"

"I'm okay, I guess, but I'll be better when Jimmy's back and we find out who's behind all this crazy stuff. Sean, somethin' was real off with your crash. I can smell it! I can't wait 'til we get to the bottom of all this foolishness."

"Billy, I hate like hell that I haven't been able to help you guys find Jimmy!"

"Hey, Sean, don't go worryin' yourself; your dad and all of us have been on the hunt. Don't feel like you're lettin' Jimmy down. You're injured, for God's sake."

To change the subject, Sean told Billy Ray, "I had a doctor here rig a contraption for my knee, so I'll be able to race in the Gator." He didn't tell Billy Ray that his doctors were really opposed to him racing with his knee injury and thought it was a crazy idea.

Billy Ray asked, "Are you sure you're not gonna go and reinjure yourself, Sean? Let's see how you're feelin' in four days, okay?"

Sean, quickly changed the subject again, and said to Billy, "How about you getting me out of the hospital for a little bit of fun tonight? I'm going stir crazy."

"Sounds interesting, Sean. Let me think about it and call you back."

"Okay," said Sean.

Billy Ray felt antsy, too. But, he was very concerned about Sean's injury and Jimmy's disappearance. Making matters worse, Billy Ray didn't know where the hell Dakota was. He couldn't ignore it any longer; she was becoming more and more distant and aloof. They had been through so much together and shared so much, including their love of stock car racing. He always thought that he had finally found a soulmate in Dakota

When Billy Ray was a young boy, he never knew who his biological father was; he was told that his real mother died giving birth to him. Being adopted into a troubled family wasn't exactly a good foundation. His adoptive mother, Annie Harper, tried to provide a loving home, but she was married to a drunk and a failure who could never get ahead. Mick Harper pickled his brain with cheap liquor and took out his frustrations on Annie and young Billy Ray. Annie did her best to act as a buffer, keeping him away from Mick's fists, but it didn't help. When he was old enough, Annie encouraged him to learn a trade and get out of the house. Billy Ray loved working on cars and found that he was very good at fixing racing engines.

He met Dakota while working as a mechanic at Burdie Graham's garage in Franklyn County, North Carolina. He remembered seeing her his first day at the garage. Burdie, a soft-hearted, salt-of-the-earth kind of guy, was telling this beautiful girl, "You're awful pretty, so wear a hat and tuck in that long black mane of yours—so the guys won't be hittin' on ya. Yer too good a mechanic for me to lose, so just pretend you're one of the boys; we'll call ya *Phil.*"

Billy Ray felt an emotional connection to her right away.

Burdie would allow them to borrow a car to go cruising on Friday nights. "As long as you don't crash 'em," he laughed with a wink.

Burdie also introduced them to the local stock car races. Burdie was a special guy, and Billy Ray and Dakota would always remember him and the time they spent working there.

He and Dakota both had had tough childhoods and had many other things in common. Billy Ray admired Dakota's burning ambition to succeed. With her as his inspiration, he could put his past behind him and create a whole new future. It didn't take long for them to fall deeply in love. She completed him, and for the first time he had someone who gave him the unconditional love he craved, so naturally, the next step was moving in together. *It's lasted all these years*, he thought.

It was getting late, and the walls seemed to be closing in on Billy Ray. He knew that he would have to press Dakota for an explanation of where the hell she'd been spending her time lately, which he dreaded. But at the moment, he had other things on his mind. The job was never too far away from his thoughts, and right now he needed to think about work as a distraction.

Billy Ray called Hank and invited him out for a drink so the two of them could talk shop. Hank was working on a new line of synthetic motor oils for race cars. Billy Ray was always interested in keeping ahead of the competition and wanted to hear what Hank had to say.

Billy Ray also remembered Sean itching to get out of the hospital for a little fun. He came up with a half-baked idea and said, "Hey, Hank! What do you think if we got Sean out of the hospital for a few hours of fun at Tito's? Then later we'll sneak him back in."

Tito's, was one of their favorite sports bars in Ormond Beach.

At first, Hank thought Billy Ray was out of his mind, but he had been lonely without Sean around, and said, "Sure! But how are we going to pull this off?"

**BILLY AND HANK** got to the hospital in record time and before going to Sean's room, which was on the first floor, they sweet-talked one of the nurses into helping them. She distracted the head nurse and the boys covered Sean with a blanket as they quickly maneuvered his wheelchair out the front entrance. Billy thought, *If Ace found out, our arses would be in a sling, as Ace would say.*

As the boys wheeled Sean into Tito's, the loud din of the crowd hurt their ears. The place was hopping! It had a well-worn look with lots of round, wooden tables and uncomfortable chairs The best thing about Tito's was the food—real guy food, like great hamburgers and fries, and to Hank's delight, the best tortilla chips and guacamole dip. The large flat screen TVs were always showing the biggest sports events: baseball, football, soccer, and of course, car racing. The jukebox was always blaring some honky-tonk melody. And what made the food taste even better and the beer go down easier were busty waitresses wearing lime green T-shirts with the name *Tito's* across their chests.

At first, Hank and Billy Ray were in a serious thinking mode, which kept them from enjoying the pretty scenery. Sean, sitting in his wheel chair, had been basking in all of the attention he was getting from attractive girls who were fussing over him because of his racing injury. They were feeding him French fries and hamburgers. He was still shaky and out of it from all of his pain medications, but he was so happy to be out of the hospital for a few hours.

In between eating and drinking their beers, Billy Ray asked Hank how the synthetic motor oil tests were going. Hank was delighted to finally have someone to talk shop, as Sean's short attention span didn't make for suitable company whenever Hank wanted to get technical. In his rapid-fire speech, Hank spent twenty minutes giving Billy Ray a dissertation on his motor oil testing at the DMS motor dynamometer lab. Somehow Billy Ray managed to keep up with Hank without yawning too much. Beers didn't seem to slow Hank down much and neither did a very pretty face. Hank turned his head just in time to see a very attractive girl being led to a nearby table. Billy Ray, following Hank's gaze, said, "Charming." They grinned at each other and ordered another round.

After several beers and feeling no pain, they decided to go out into the night air and cruise around town. Hank helped Sean into Billy Ray's truck. Hank was untwisting his seat belt when he felt something under his seat. He reached down and scooped it up to discover that they were binoculars. "Wow, these are cool. I never saw anything like them before. Where did you get them?"

"Check them out," Billy Ray said. "Ace gave them to me. You can see in the dark with them."

"Yeah," said Hank. "Ace always gives out great gadgets. These are great!"

While they were cruising, a slightly intoxicated Billy Ray made a quick turn, squealing the tires, and said, "Hey, I know this shtreet. Benecio Villereal lives on this block. I hear he keepssh a lab down in his basement. Let's check it out."

Billy Ray pulled his truck over and parked near Villereal's house but made sure it was out of sight. The lights were on in Benecio's large, white, two-story Colonial home, which looked very out of place in Florida. The massive shrubs and tall trees covering up much of the house looked like they were there for privacy.

"Somebody must be home," Billy Ray whispered to Hank. "Bring the binoculars ssho we can get a closer look... S-Sean, you stay and be our look out, okay?"

"Sure," said Sean laughing at Billy Ray's slurred speech. Sean laughed again as he watched both boys, tipsy from the beers, get out of the truck.

Billy Ray said, "Hank, now, we haff to be quiet—shh, cuz we're spyin' on wuzhizface."

Even drunk, Billy Ray couldn't switch off his focus from work. He was always curious about an expert like Benecio Villereal, who also owned the VRL Petro-Chemical Company in Texas. VRL specialized in high performance lubricants. They produced a line of synthetic oil additives that boosted a race car's horsepower. Engine builders like

Billy Ray and Hank were obsessed with finding any way to reduce power robbing engine friction.

"I bet that's how Villereal/Clayton is building such a strong motor for Carl Zimmer," said Billy Ray.

Hank began processing the possibilities and said, "Yes, the power curve must be awesome. That's what I've been working on."

"Yeah, Ace is impressed with your work in the shop. He thinks you're a freakin' genius."

Hank nodded, appreciating the compliment.

Billy Ray scanned Villereal's house to see if anything was going on. Just then, a car pulled out of his garage. Billy Ray jumped out of sight, grabbing Hank and pushing him down on the ground. As the car sped away, Billy Ray got up and started pacing.

"Jeez, where would he be going this late at night and in such a hurry? What the hell sh-should we do?"

"Hey! I got an idea! Letsh follow him," said Hank.

He and Hank ran back to the truck and told Sean what had happened. Without missing a beat they all agreed to follow Villereal.

## CHAPTER FOURTEEN

# THE CHASE IS ON

B eing the only sober one, Sean became the designated driver. He told Billy Ray that maybe he'd be better off sitting 'shotgun'. Billy Ray agreed and Hank helped Sean move into the driver's seat, and propped up his braced leg. They took off after Villereal, now that their curiosity had gotten the better of them. Unfortunately for Billy Ray and Hank, so did the alcohol. But thankfully, they knew Sean could drive Billy Ray's truck, even blindfolded. Sean stayed back far enough so as to not let on that he was tailing him.

They followed the route Villereal took, and they couldn't believe their eyes when they saw him park at one of Clayton's warehouses on the outskirts of town. They stayed back and out of sight.

Hank said, "He's probably going to his lab to work on some of his experiments."

Billy Ray said, "What? How do *you* know that's where his lab is?"

"...Ummm... I just know," said Hank.

Sean said, "Hey guys, as long as we're here, we should hatch a plan to see what's going on in there. I vote that we sneak in and see what Uncle Benecio is up to?"

Billy Ray joked, "Yeah, right. You'll just roll in with your wheelchair and say hello to your Uncle." They all laughed.

Hank said, "There are security cameras all around. How about one of us sneaks in and another one throws a rock at the camera?"

"Well, okay, but we might need to cause a distraction in case we have to get out of there in a hurry," said Billy Ray.

"Leave that to me. I'll sneak into the lab and look around, and maybe I can find something to cause a little smoke to get everyone out," said Hank.

Billy Ray was all in black which made him easy to camouflage. Sean parked out of sight and away from the cameras. Hank found a big rock and hurled it at the security camera closest to the front of the warehouse. Billy Ray looked up and saw lights on the fourth floor. He sprinted over to the side of the building and finding it open, snuck in. He quietly ran up the stairs to the fourth floor and held his breath as he opened the door and prayed a security alarm wouldn't go off.

Sean was sitting in the truck, watching with Billy Ray's binoculars.

Billy Ray sprang into action and ran down the hallway toward the light. He thought he heard someone moving around in one of the rooms, and then he stopped cold. He heard someone moaning, and it seemed to be coming from inside a room a few doors away. Seeing the door ajar, he pushed it open and saw Jimmy Stanton tied up on the floor, obviously drugged and incoherent. He looked around the room. A closed-circuit TV camera was aimed at Jimmy. Billy Ray couldn't believe that this was where they had been keeping Jimmy. "What the hell's going on here!" he whispered to himself. Billy Ray's heart was beating so loudly he thought it was going to explode. He was stunned. It was a mystery to him why Jimmy was being held there like a prisoner in Clayton's warehouse. *Was Clayton crazy,* he thought?

He looked down the corridor to see if anybody was coming. He wondered if Villereal or Clayton or both were behind this terrible scheme of Jimmy's kidnapping and his imprisonment. Billy Ray figured that they had someone guarding Jimmy, and that he'd be coming back any minute. He turned around and whispered, "Jimmy...Jimmy, can you hear me?"

Jimmy stirred on the floor. He mumbled, "Sean...get me outta here."

Shocked, Billy Ray thought, *Jesus, the kid is delirious.*

Billy Ray had to get Jimmy out of there. He thought about what he needed to do and realized he needed help. He didn't think he could pull it off by himself. Billy Ray remembered the idea Hank mentioned in the truck. He said to Jimmy, "Stanton, hold on, I'll be right back!" He rushed down the corridor toward a room that looked like a lab, trying to come up with a plan. He'd have to think fast before Benecio or someone else would discover him. He wished Hank was with him.

Just then, he heard footsteps and looked up and there was Hank.

"Whew! Jeez, you scared the hell out of me, but you are a sight for sore eyes," whispered Billy. "Quick, we have to create a diversion. Jimmy is being held here. He's in terrible shape."

Hank shrieked, "What? Jimmy's here?"

"Yeah, quick, we need that diversion you were talking about to get him out of here. He's all tied up!"

Hank looked around the lab and said. "I got just the thing to stir things up. A couple of smoke pots should do the trick. And when the fire alarm goes off, we'll grab Jimmy and run like hell."

Hank made the smoke pots and set them off. Moments later, the alarm bells clanged as smoke filled the hallway. Billy Ray went running down the hall yelling, "Fire! Fire! Help!"

Jimmy's guard ran out into the smoke-filled hall in a panic and bumped into Billy Ray who shouted, "Come quick! The lab is on fire! Help me put it out."

The guard started coughing from the smoke. "Not me, buddy," he said. "I don't get paid enough to burn!" He backed away from Billy Ray and quickly ran out of the building.

Billy Ray and Hank ran into Jimmy's room and knocked over the security camera. Hank quickly pulled out his pocket knife and began cutting through the bindings that held Jimmy. He shouted, "Jimmy— Jimmy, wake up, boy!" Billy Ray shook him.

Jimmy thought he was hallucinating. "Sean, is that you?"

Billy Ray grabbed Jimmy and shook him. "Jimmy, come on now. Wake up, Jimmy!" He slapped Jimmy's cheek a few times to make him more alert.

Jimmy moved slowly at first and then shook his head to shake off the stupor he was in. In his foggy haze, he kept questioning his eyesight. Then he fell back into his stupor, mumbling, "Sean...got to tell Sean."

Hank cut off the last restraint and Billy Ray lifted Jimmy up into his arms.

Desperately trying to keep Jimmy awake enough to get him to walk, Billy Ray ended up carrying him down four smoke-filled staircases, with Hank right behind them silently praying they wouldn't be caught. They heard loud voices coming from another part of the building. By then, security must have been alerted that something was going on. The piercing loud clanging of alarm bells rang out. Panicked, the boys struggled with Jimmy as they were going down the last set of stairs getting closer to the landing. Hank heard footsteps approaching and men shouting to each other, and yelled out to Billy Ray, "Let's get the hell out of here! They're coming!"

Waiting at the side door of the warehouse, was Sean with Billy Ray's truck. Hank and Billy Ray carefully lifted Jimmy into the back seat and covered him with a blanket. "Punch it, Sean!" Billy Ray yelled.

As they took off in the truck with Jimmy, Sean looked in the rear view mirror and saw men running out of the warehouse. But one man in particular looked familiar and as Sean narrowed his focus he clearly saw Benecio Villereal. Billy Ray, Sean, and Hank were silent for a minute trying to process everything.

Finally Sean broke the silence, "What the hell just happened? You found JP in my grandfather's warehouse? And was that Uncle Benecio running out?" Nobody answered him. The whole thing was too shocking.

They drove straight to the hospital and snuck Sean back into his room and then they left Jimmy in the ER, while Billy Ray called Ace in New York.

**ACE WAS SO** furious he couldn't contain his anger. Was his father-in-law and best friend involved in the deadly plot to kidnap and drug Jimmy, not to mention the taser assault on his own son? Ace was seething. He sat up in his chair and thought, *I have to call a lot of*

*people now, to let them know we got Jimmy back safe and alive.* Fortunately, he and Connor were planning to meet for lunch in an hour at Mickel's, a popular Manhattan restaurant on 55th Street right off Fifth Avenue. He and Connor met there every week. He'd share the great news about Jimmy with him there.

He called Jimmy's father first and told him Jimmy was safe. He assured Mr. Stanton that he would have Jimmy call as soon as he was feeling better.

Taylor was next on the list. For her, he would have to revise the back story of where they found Jimmy. There was no way Ace was going to reveal to his wife that her father and maybe Benecio were responsible for Jimmy's kidnapping.

Handling Taylor was always a chore, but Ace was an expert at dealing with his wife's quirks. She didn't handle bad news well and usually did her best to put any nasty business out of her mind. But Jimmy was an exception. When she heard he went missing, she worried about him like a mother hen.

Ace was happy to break the news to her that they had found Jimmy in an old abandoned building on the outskirts of town. He also explained, truthfully, that Jimmy was being taken to a nearby clinic for medical attention.

"Oh, honee, that's wonderful," she said. "Where will Jimmy go when he's released from the clinic?"

"I thought our condo would be a good place for him to be safe until the Gator 500."

Taylor said, "In that case, I'll have the guest room made up for him now."

"Thanks deah," said Ace. Ace was hoping that JP might be well enough to race in the Gator 500 in just four days. Ace said to Taylor, "He's a strong boy. If I know Jimmy, he'll try his damndest to build up his strength, so he'll be able to drive."

After Ace finished his phone calls, he began to go over all the events in his mind. He wondered whether Clayton also had something to do with Sean's car going haywire and crashing. If Taylor ever knew what her father was up to, it would absolutely destroy her.

This was the same man who had welcomed Ace into his family; and set Ace up in the Devlin Media conglomerate. The man had gone mad. Jimmy would have to be sworn to secrecy; he could never breathe a word of it to Taylor or anyone else.

The one person Ace always thought he could trust was his old friend Benecio Villereal. He, Taylor, and Benecio had all been close friends at Harvard. Ace and Benecio served in the Gulf War together and always watched out for each other. "Uncle Benecio" was godfather to Ace and Taylor's children. He wasn't so sure now after what Sean had told him about the strange look Benecio had on his face when he came running out of Clayton's warehouse staring at them as they sped away with Jimmy. Ace would have to tread lightly with Benecio and launch his own private investigation into this whole sabotage matter without letting his best friend know.

Jimmy was the one who would need to be watched. He was like another son to Ace. Ace was worried that Jimmy would suffer post-traumatic stress, after his horrible ordeal of being kidnapped, drugged, and tied-up for several days.

## CHAPTER FIFTEEN

# GOOD MORNING, MRS. DEVLIN

It was late when Billy Ray finally got home after rescuing Jimmy. He was dog-tired and knew he only had a few hours to get some sleep before he had to pick up Taylor early in the morning. He'd hoped he'd see Dakota there waiting for him, but their place was empty. Feeling bone-tired weary, emotionally drained, and sick to his stomach from too much beer, Billy Ray tumbled into their empty bed. Sleep eluded him, though, and he decided to wait up until Dakota got home. The thought of losing her was horrible enough, but every call not answered, every text ignored, the everyday stuff they weren't doing together were like spikes to his heart. He curled up on the bed, trying to comfort his bruised soul. He was afraid his whole world was coming apart.

Just then, the sound of a car approaching outside broke the pre-dawn silence. Billy Ray sat up to listen. He hoped it was Dakota. His heart jumped when he heard Dakota come into the RV, and he whispered, "Thank you, God." He pretended to be asleep to avoid a confrontation. He heard her go into the bathroom and turn on the shower, and then he finally fell asleep.

He woke up around 5:00 a.m. and felt like road kill and wished he had gotten more sleep. His stomach was in knots, and he felt like the air in the room had become oppressive. An eerie stillness took over, and he could swear that thick currents of electricity were bouncing off Dakota's body, like something very bad was about to happen. She was lying next to him, asleep. Mornings used to be their favorite time to make love, but now it felt unnatural and awkward. Before forcing himself out of bed, he looked at her longingly, remembering how she moved and how much pleasure they both got every time they made love. He tried to memorize her beautiful face—her almond shaped deep blue eyes and small ruby lips, all framed in a perfectly symmetrical face. His heart was heavy, and the thought of losing her was ripping his guts apart, but he had to tear himself away to pick up Taylor. After doing his morning rituals quietly, so as not to wake her up, he wrote Dakota a note saying that he and Mrs. Devlin were going to pick Sean up from the hospital; he added 'Please call me. We need to talk!' He wished he could escape from his enormous pain...but he couldn't. He would never let anyone get this close to him again.

Keeping his promise to Ace, a sleepy Billy Ray Harper pulled his truck into the parking lot of the Devlins' Ormond Beach condo just before sunrise. Checking his watch, he still had a minute or two before he had to pick up the boss's wife at 6:30 a.m. He relaxed for a moment and sipped a cup of coffee. He could barely focus and keep his mind alert, and the last thing in the world Billy Ray wanted to do was accompany Mrs. Devlin to the hospital to pick up Sean. Not that he wasn't happy that his good friend was getting released, but he just couldn't reprogram his emotions.

Billy Ray knocked on the door at the Devlins' condo. He heard a few muffled voices, and then Taylor Devlin opened the door. She was still a very attractive woman for being in her late forties, with long honey-blonde hair and a knock-out figure *but definitely not my taste,* he thought. She was wearing a lilac-colored halter top in her foxy Hollywood style.

"Good morning, Billy Ray."

"Um, g'morning, Mrs. Devlin, ma'am. I'm here to take you to the hospital. It will be great to have Sean back. I sure have missed him!" His fingers were crossed knowing he was lying after seeing Sean the night before.

Hearing voices again inside the condo, Billy Ray asked, "Do you have company?" Taylor reacted strangely, trying to distract Billy Ray. "Oh, honee, that was just one of Ace's bodyguards keeping li'l ole me company. Pay him no mind." She shoved Billy Ray out into the hall-way, continuing, "You know, honee...with all this nasty business going on, Ace just wanted to make sure I was safe. Isn't that sweet of him? By the way, we are so proud of you boys for finding Jimmy. It was just terrible what he went through, but thank God he's gonna be all right." Taylor smiled sweetly and said, "Just let me go change, Billy Ray. I'll be right back."

Outside the condo, a pickup truck and an SUV crept to a halt just past the parking lot, out of view of Billy Ray's truck. The tinted windows made it impossible to see who was inside. Billy Ray led Taylor to his truck and held the door as she climbed in. Two men in the truck observed Billy Ray and Taylor; one of them grabbed his cell phone and said, "Yeah, they just got in Harper's truck." He listened to the response, and then said, "Okay, so you want us to just scare them and not hurt anybody? Ya okay with this?" The person on the phone got angry and shouted more orders. He answered, "Okay, but we can't guarantee that nobody will get hurt. You know what happens in a car crash? Yes, they are leaving now. Okay. Yer the boss!" He closed his cell phone and said to the driver, "Follow Harper's truck!"

Meanwhile, Hank pulled Sean's SUV into the hospital parking lot. He figured Sean would be more comfortable in a big car where he could stretch out his bum leg. Ace had told him to stay in touch on the DMS company two-way radio-phone. After Jimmy's kidnapping, it was only natural for Ace to worry about the safety of his crew in addition to the drivers.

Billy Ray and Taylor sat in silence at a long red light. Taylor turned and studied Billy Ray's features. Taylor was the kind of woman who appreciated a good looking man. Never mind the fact that she was more than sixteen years older. Pretty boys were always fair game to Taylor.

Billy Ray, had a swagger about him that attracted a lot of attention from men *and* women. He was tall and lanky, with dark wavy hair and dark almond shaped eyes that seemed to pierce your soul. As Taylor looked at him, she thought about kissing those lips. To break his spell of perfection, there was a deep scar over his left eyebrow. Her eyes followed his profile downward. She sighed, thinking he could fill out his jeans like no one else. Muscles bulged everywhere on that fine young body, and he had some interesting tattoos on his arm. One of them caught her eye. It looked like a rising phoenix. Taylor wondered what the bird stood for. Lost in a daydream, Taylor began to fantasize about making love to Billy Ray. Benecio Villereal had that sexy magic too. She put that thought right out of her mind. They were over a long time ago. Although he was in his late 40's, Taylor thought Benecio was still a very handsome man. He was tall, athletic looking and very powerfully built. His face had angular features with interesting lines. His penetrating deep brown eyes seemed to conceal a lifetime of deep sorrow. He wore his thick black wavy hair slicked back.

Taylor loved to compete with other women, and knowing that Billy Ray was living with Dakota Philips made him even more tempting.

"Billy Ray, tell me about your life before Devlin Racing," she said.

The light turned green and Billy Ray turned left to head for the highway. He was surprised by the personal question and stalled to gather his thoughts. When Billy Ray got nervous, he often talked too much, and soon he was telling her about his terrible childhood. He did not notice the pickup truck shadowing them from behind as he continued to talk. He repeated the story the Harpers told him about his past and how they came to adopt him.

He said to Taylor, "I found out from my adoptive mother that my real mother died when I was born. I'm still trying to find out who my biological father is. Actually, Dakota is helping me by researching special websites online." He turned to Taylor and said, "I remember being told my birth mother's name was Rosalinda something."

When Taylor heard that name, her mouth dropped open in horror and her face turned pale. "Oh my God, Billy! Stop the truck," she exclaimed. She unbuckled her seat belt in her panic and began to open the door while Billy Ray struggled to get out of traffic and pull to the side of the road.

"What's the matter, Mrs. D?"

"I need to get out," she said. "I feel sick!"

Taylor flung the door open while the truck was still moving and was about to jump out when *Crash!* The guys in the pickup truck chose that moment to ram Billy Ray's truck. The impact knocked Taylor back into the door jamb, and Billy Ray grabbed her arm and pulled her into the truck just before the door slammed shut. Taylor's head struck the dashboard. Holding her hand to her bruised head, she cried out, "Holy Pete!"

Billy Ray shouted, "Mrs. Devlin!"

Taylor held her hand to her head and clenched her teeth in anger. She looked over her shoulder to see what hit them. "I'm okay, Billy. Keep drivin'. It looks like this guy isn't through with us."

Billy Ray looked out his side view mirror and saw the pickup truck speeding up for another attack; he looked into his other mirror and noticed the SUV also gaining on them. He said, "Jeez! There's two of 'em!" Billy Ray pushed the gas pedal to the floorboard. The motor roared, spinning his dual rear tires, kicking up the gravel like buckshot at the two vehicles closing in on them.

Taylor's blood was running hot. "Yeah! Give it to 'em, Billy!" She had already forgotten her distress when Billy had mentioned the name of his biological mother. The stones peppered the pickup truck behind them, but it didn't stop them. Taylor looked out the back window and yelled, "Billy, they're coming again!"

Billy Ray shouted back, "You better buckle yourself up—or would you prefer to drive?" *Crash!* The SUV rammed them from behind.

"No honee, y'all doin' just fine!" She quickly buckled up and said, "I'll be your co-pilot!"

Billy Ray raced ahead, but the SUV kept tailing right behind them. He weaved in and out of traffic, but that didn't seem to deter them. Taylor was more mad than scared. As a former race car driver, she still had nerves of steel and prompted Billy Ray to make one maneuver after another. She picked up the two-way radio-phone and pressed the walkie-talkie key.

"Ace, honee?"

Ace radioed back, "Taylor, is that you?"

"Yes dear. A bunch of country boys want to tangle with Billy and me. They are trying to wreck us."

Hank, who was waiting at the hospital with Sean, heard the alarm over their radio. "H-hand me that radio!" Sean said. Hank fumbled to get it out of his belt holster.

Sean keyed up, "Mom? Are you all right? Where are you? We'll come and get you."

Ace responded, "Now Sean, you were just in a wreck. You stay the hell out of this."

Sean ignored Ace and repeated himself, "W-where are you, Mom? I'll meet up with you guys."

Billy Ray grabbed the phone from Taylor and said, "We need all the help we can get." He keyed up the mic and said, "Sean, we're on the highway southbound just a few miles from the hospital. Ace, we're gonna need some heat to deal with these boys."

Ace responded, "Yeah, I heah ya. I know who these boys are. See if you can dodge them until I get Earl Hammond on the line."

Sean keyed in, "B-Billy, keep heading to the hospital, and we'll come north to intercept."

Billy Ray responded, "Roger that, Sean."

"Hank, g-get me to the car," Sean said.

Hank pushed his wheelchair toward the exit. "Hey Sean, you thinking of doing the driving?"

"Who better to drive?"

Hank cackled, "You got a point!"

Hank helped Sean ease into the driver's seat and buckled his seat belt. He helped Sean position his braced leg and then ran around to the passenger side as Sean revved the SUV's powerful engine. He barely got in before Sean floored it, throwing him back into his seat. They screeched out of the parking lot. "Hank, find out where B-Billy is now," Sean said as he raced to the highway.

Taylor responded over the two-way radio-phone, "We're about a half mile away, honee, and we're coming fast."

Hank spotted Billy Ray's flashing lights and yelled, "There they are, Sean! And those must be the bad guys behind them; they're coming up fast. What are you gonna do?"

"Henry," Sean said, "you are about to see some *real* driving!" He jerked the wheel to the left to spin his SUV around one hundred eighty degrees. Then he powered into a slide while accelerating into the southbound lane behind the other SUV that was chasing Billy Ray. Other traffic scattered with horns honking as Sean pulled up to the SUV's bumper. The driver tried his best to shake Sean, but he couldn't get away. He slammed his brakes to back-ram Sean but did little damage to the heavy duty bumper on the front of Sean's SUV.

Sean said, "Okay, let's put this guy out of his m-misery."

Hank looked over at Sean and asked, "What are you gonna do?"

Sean grinned at Hank. "S-something Jimmy t-taught me. He got this trick from his buddy in the Atlanta police department." Sean dropped his SUV into a lower gear and accelerated to catch up to the other SUV. He waited for the right moment and then turned the wheel sharply to the left, knocking the other SUV into a tailspin. *Wham!* The SUV crashed into a guard rail and flipped over, sliding to a rest. Sean said, "That's one down."

Hank shook his head in amazement. "How did you do that?"

Sean laughed and said, "And you c-call yourself an engineer?"

Billy Ray grabbed the two-way radio-phone from Taylor again. "Sean, I can't shake this guy in the pickup. Let's do a squeeze play and put a stop to this."

Sean confirmed Billy Ray's thought. "You w-want me to b-block him from behind and lock bumpers?"

Billy Ray said, "Yeah, sort of a rolling roadblock."

"Roger that, B-Billy."

Ace keyed in, "You guys all right?"

Taylor took the radio-phone and responded, "Everything is okay, honee. We just have to do a little mopping up."

Ace radioed back, "I talked to Earl Hammond. He's sending some troopers to help you. He told me there was already a call about an SUV that flipped over. Would that be your handiwork?"

"Oh, honee, we'll talk about it later. Sean is about to do"—*Thump!*—"something."

Taylor looked over her shoulder and said, "Okay, Billy Ray, Sean pushed him right over your back bumper. He's got nowhere to go. You can slow it down now."

Billy Ray braked all three vehicles to a smooth stop. The troopers rolled up just in time to keep the guys in the pickup from making an escape. Trooper Earl Hammond pulled up beside Sean's SUV and shouted, "You Devlins sure start making trouble early in the morning. Lucky your old man talks fast or we'd be tossing all yer asses in the slammer—kit and caboodle."

Taylor walked up to Hammond's car and leaned in the window. "Now Earl, is that any way to be talking to a lady?"

Hammond, now blushing, said to Taylor, "Sorry, ma'am. I'm glad everybody is safe."

Taylor gave Earl her best sexy smile. "Why, thank you, Earl. That's right kind of ya." Taylor loved to pour on her southern accent for effect whenever she needed to. She turned around to Billy Ray who was talking to Sean and Hank. "C'mon boys! Let's all go for breakfast; it's on me!"

"Roger that," said Sean. "But first I have to g-go and change my underwear."

Everyone laughed, including Earl. "Hey, boys," he said, "make me proud on Saturday, okay?"

"Will do," said Sean. "And thanks, Earl, for all your help!

## CHAPTER SIXTEEN

# *ACE VS. CLAYTON*

### *A FEW DAYS BEFORE GATOR 500*

Look, Clayton, I have the goods on you: kidnapping, conspiracy, reckless endangerment, and perhaps even attempted murder. The only person keeping your arse out of jail is me. And if you want to keep it that way, you will do exactly what I say." Ace Devlin was angry enough to kill. The only thing holding him back was the fact that his family was out of harm's way and he was holding all the right cards to do as he pleased. Ace, Connor and his family, Avery, and Sekou would all be flying in for the Gator 500. But right then he was back at his desk in his New York City office, waiting for a response from his father-in-law on the phone. Everything was silent except for the sound of clinking glass.

Taylor Clayton Sr., very tall with a full head of silver hair, slim and sun-kissed with craggy skin, was still very attractive for a man in his seventies. He was in his dark green library, standing in front of his curved mahogany bar, while trying to pour himself a scotch. He had a panicked expression on his face. He picked up the phone and cleared his throat. Feigning ignorance, he said, "Why Ace, I don't know what you're talking about, son. What's all this about?"

Ace knew the old coot well enough to know when he was lying.

Ace got personal. "Clayton, you almost killed your daughter today!"

"What? What are you talking about?"

"You sent a bunch of thugs to crash into Billy Ray; she was in the truck with him."

Clayton was genuinely shocked at the news. "I did no such thing, Ace. I swear to you..."

"They were the same guys who kidnapped Jimmy Stanton. The cops have them now. Seems they had a lot to say."

Clayton gulped his scotch and started to think hard. Sweat was beading on his upper lip; a wild look came into his eyes. He was confused." Why would I send somebody to hurt my daughter and Billy Ray?"

Ace continued, "Look, Clayton, business is business, and at the track, we all pull stunts in friendly competition to keep things interesting, but you are slipping, old man!"

Clayton defended himself quickly, and said, "Ace, I had nothing to do with sending somebody to hurt Billy Ray and Taylor. She's my little girl. I just wouldn't do such a thing. I have protected her all her life. I saw to it that she was with the right people and she was taken care of. You came to me for my blessing when you wanted to marry her, and I gave it, remember? Ace, you have to believe me—I wouldn't do anything to hurt Taylor or Billy Ray or anybody else for that matter."

Ace sensed Clayton's sincerity, but his anger still made him skeptical. "Look, you sonuvabitch! You kidnapped Jimmy Stanton and pumped him full of drugs. You could have killed him. What the hell were you thinking?"

Clayton found his stride and turned on the smooth talk. "Now, now Ace, calm yourself. There was no harm done, was there? You found Stanton, didn't you?" Clayton was a genius at getting out of a bad situation. "We were just having a little fun with you. So we snatched your driver. What's the harm in that?"

Ace was ready to blow. "What's the harm? Clayton, do you even heah yourself? Are you out of your mind? They tasered Sean! They set Jimmy up and then kidnapped him. And I can't prove it now, but I'm convinced you had something to do with Sean's crash. Clayton, people are getting hurt. *My* people. Hell...*your* people! *Family!* What are you, some kind of *monster*? You have to be stopped."

Fear began to grip Clayton. It looked like this time he had to account for his actions. "What are you going to do, son?"

Ace knew what he wanted to do, but he had to think this out carefully. There were other things to consider, other people that would be affected by his actions. He drew a deep breath and sighed.

"This is what you have to do if you want to keep your butt out of jail: I don't want Taylor to evah find out what you did. It would tear this family apart! It's bad enough that Sean, Billy Ray and Jimmy suspect you. You are going to clean up your mess and get your bums out of jail and pay their fines. I'll make sure they are not charged with anything. You know I got enough on you to throw the whole lot of you in jail for attempted murdah. You're going to pretend that nothing happened between us, and you're going to show up at family functions and act like everything is just fine. I won't have Taylor or the rest of my family suspecting a thing. You are going to stay away from my people, and if there are any retaliations, I swear, Clayton, I will blow you out of the water, father-in-law or not."

"Okay, Ace, you have my promise, and I'll swear to it on Mariella's grave."

## CHAPTER SEVENTEEN
# MELTDOWN

Taylor Clayton Sr. was fit to be tied. He had just walked into his library, tired after a long day at his warehouse office, when he was ambushed by the call from his son-in-law. Ace was relentless in his accusations. Clayton detested being found out. He knew he had gone over the line. He continued to pace back and forth like a caged animal. Clayton just wanted to get Sean and Jimmy Stanton out of the way so Zimmer could win the Gator. He took another swallow of scotch. "Damn!" he shouted angrily. Beating his forehead repeatedly with the heel of his hand, he yelled, "Stupid, stupid, stupid!" He was trying his best to make sense out of the debacle he had created for his family and drivers.

He wondered how he was going to square this disaster with Ace. He felt tired and depressed, which was a new feeling for him, and he was not the sort of man who took defeat well. He hoped a nap would help all this unpleasantness disappear.

Thinking about his girlfriend, the new love of his life, he stretched his long legs out on his large leather sofa and let his mind wander. Could she have been behind this latest disaster? *What have I done? I have created a monster. I still love her, damn it! I'll have to regain the upper hand,* and then Clayton drifted off to sleep.

## CHAPTER EIGHTEEN

# BACK ON TRACK

## SATURDAY: DAY OF THE GATOR 500 RACE

Sean stubbornly refused to drop out of the race despite his doctor's warning about his injured knee. "Do what it takes to stabilize my leg so I can drive!" he ordered. Considering that he needed to operate the clutch pedal, they rigged a brace that pivoted at the knee joint and gave him the support he needed, so as not to reinjure himself. The doctor warned him that it might not get him through the extremes of the race and asked him to reconsider his craziness. Sean tested the rig in physical therapy and felt confident he could withstand the pain for the four hour race.

Nothing was going to prevent Sean from racing in the Gator 500. Taylor drove him to the Ormond Beach International Speedway. Connor and Ace wanted to make sure that he would have plenty of time to glad-hand the fans and put a positive spin on his knee injury for the media. Strategically sitting on top of a big cooler, he waved hello to the crowds of fans and tried hard to reassure everybody that he was on the mend and would be able to race.

It was his third Gator 500. While he was in the hospital, Sean had an epiphany. Maybe it was the endless moments of pin-drop silence in the middle of the night, or a little help from his meds, but whatever it was, a wave of clarity suddenly swept over him bringing his life into focus. He didn't have anything to prove anymore! He finally understood his mother's words: '*Sean, you have no competition if you always believe you're number one.*' What a burden it had been for him, always having to be the best in racing or anything else he strived for, probably overcompensating for his stutter. He had lived his life trying to please his family and everyone else, and he finally realized that with all of his successes, like winning several PMRA championships, it felt hollow. Daniella was the first person to make him face the truth and take stock of his life. What she said resonated in him. She said, '*Sean, I will always love you, whether you win or lose. It's you I love, not your trophies.*' Then she added the kicker: '*You must always be true to yourself.*'

He realized for the first time that he had to start living his life for himself, writing his own rules and not living by someone else's. He had already made up his mind that he would stay in the race with his injured knee and do the best he could. He would really try not to make any unnecessary moves or take any risks that would put him or anyone else in danger. He wouldn't have to conquer the world—just stay the course.

Sean favored his injured left knee as he slowly eased himself into his new #17 car. He had to position that leg as best he could. He then adjusted his black shaded visor to shield his eyes from the bright Florida sun. Starting third from the front of the line, he was behind his old rival Carl Zimmer in the #41 car, who held pole position. Dakota Philips, in her #23 car, was also in front of Sean. DMS mechanics had discovered a last minute problem with Jimmy's original #27 car, so his replacement car had to start at the back of the pack. It would be a tall order for Jimmy to make his way through all the traffic, but then, Jimmy was known for his past experience racing through traffic back in Georgia (ask any Atlanta cop!).

Sean liked the way his car responded and made a mental note to thank the crew for all their hard work. Finally, the pace car exited the track, and the entire raceway reverberated with the sound of forty-three cars accelerating toward the waving green flag, signaling the start of the Gator 500. Everybody in the stands and around the track was on their feet waving and cheering as the cars bore down on turn one. Immediately, Sean noted the difference in traction he was getting on the recently repaved track surface. But the sun was bearing down and the track was heating up fast. Billy Ray was stationed in his perch at the #17 pit area, barking orders into his headset mic. Sean felt his heart go through its initial start-of-race arrhythmia. "Hey there, Billy, let's show 'em how it's done."

Billy Ray spoke into the mic, saying, "Good luck, Sean! I won't say 'break a leg' for luck, though!"

"Very funny," said Sean.

The car was strong and gripped well. Dakota was already at work trying to take the lead from Zimmer. Sean opted for a lower groove and began his challenge on both Dakota and Carl. Not surprising to Sean, Zimmer's car had great speed on the straightaways, but he seemed to bog down on the turns. Sean figured his only chance to catch Zimmer was to drive hard into and out of the turns. This put a lot of wear and tear on the tires, but once Sean was out front, he would put less strain on his knee; he really wanted to walk away with the race in his favor.

Sean said to Billy Ray over the radio, "The car is handling well, Billy! Great job, you guys." But just as he said it, he felt his front tires break loose as Dakota crossed in front of him and bumped the right front corner of his car. Billy Ray heard Sean's radio crackle, "Fuckin'-A! What the hell is she doing?"

That maneuver put Sean into a smoky slide sideways up the track, but he managed to turn into the slide and regain control. He was heading toward the wall in turn three but the bank in the turn helped him to pull the car around the turn. Rocketing out of turn four to regain his lost position, Sean radioed, "Man, I got nothing but greasy rubber, Billy. I'm gonna need four tires."

Billy Ray said, "Roger that. Can you hold out for a caution?"

Sean responded, "Well, I feel a vibration coming from the right rear, and the front end is just plowing into the turns now. Can you have the spotter check the rear tire for a flat?"

Al, the team spotter, called in from his position high in the stands, "I got you covered, Sean. Looks like the rear tire is holding. I don't think yer going flat. That Phil, what the...!"

"You got that right, Al," Sean retorted.

"Okay, gentlemen," said Billy Ray. "Let's keep it civil. Sean, you got a race to win. Focus on keeping that car in one piece."

"Roger that, Billy."

"By the way, how are you doing?" Billy Ray said as cryptically as possible, not to let on to radio eavesdroppers he was concerned about Sean's leg.

Sean hesitated but then said, "We're okay."

While Dakota and Carl Zimmer continued to trade places for the lead, Jimmy was wheeling his way from the back of the pack and rapidly approaching Sean who was holding his own at fifteenth position, in desperate need for new tires. Jimmy dove down to the inside lane when all of a sudden, a couple of cars behind him made contact with each other and clipped the outside wall just past turn four. Chaos ensued as the pack of cars behind Jimmy spun out while survivors dodged the wrecks and gained position. The yellow caution flag came out—good news for Sean.

"Pit, pit, pit!" radioed Billy Ray. "Give him four tires!"

Sean peeled off the track for pit road along with just about everybody else while the track officials cleared off the crash debris. Sean skidded his car to a stop in the #17 pit stall, and his pit crew hustled over the wall with tires in hand. *Zzzzip, zzzip, zzzip* went the pneumatic wrenches, loosening the lug nuts. Like a machine, the crew pulled the old tires off and threw the new tires on in a matter of seconds. At the same time, they refueled the car, cleared debris from the grill, and checked the front end for damage where Dakota's car had bumped Sean. Just a minor scrape.

Billy Ray radioed, "Go! Go! Go!" and Sean laid a patch of rubber in his hurry to get out of the pit before Dakota and Carl Zimmer did. It was going to be close. Hopefully Sean could reclaim a better position behind the pace car while the caution flag was still out. Zimmer and Dakota were in third and fourth position, but Sean advanced ten positions to the number five position. Jimmy pitted well too; he advanced to the seventh position. Ace and Connor were elated that all three of the DMS cars were now in the top ten; any one of them were in contention for the win.

93

Buzzy Durant in the #22 car made the most of his situation. Four laps before the caution, he pitted for two right side tires and fuel. By not entering the pit during the caution, he recovered from a deficit of a whole lap and claimed the lead away from Zimmer. He only had two fresh tires, so he would have to fight to keep his lead position from the others who had a chance of overtaking him on four new tires that would offer better traction.

With the #17 car back to its full potential, Sean was not concerned about Buzzy's lead. It was a huge gamble for Buzzy, and it was still early enough in the race to wait Buzzy out until his two tires no longer had the grip to hold the lead. Sean's real threat remained with Carl Zimmer, Dakota, and his own aching leg, which was beginning to spasm from overwork.

The race restarted. "Damn!" Sean cursed as he missed a shift. Jimmy took advantage of Sean's error and zoomed past him. Sean's radio crackled with Billy Ray's voice. "What's up, Sean? Is something wrong with the car?"

Sean responded, after getting up to speed, "Naw, dammit! I missed a shift. Sorry about that, Billy. I'll try to make up for it."

Jimmy drafted his car behind Dakota to get the momentum he needed for his next move. He got his chance, coming out of turn two on the inside lane, and shot past Dakota, Zimmer, and then Durant. The fans were standing on their seats, screaming in unison.

The announcer on the track public address system yelled, "Did you see that?" He was so shocked, he was reduced to laughter. "That was Jimmy Stanton, ladies and gentlemen! Jim-my Stan-ton in the #27 car takes the lead!" The crowd roared so loud Jimmy actually heard them cheering him as he raced past the stands unchallenged. The announcer continued, "Jimmy came all the way from the back of the pack to finally take the lead! Let's hear it for Jimmy Stanton!" The crowd roared with renewed energy.

Sean, still six cars behind the lead, witnessed that ridiculous move by his best buddy. He said aloud, "That was *sick*! Way to go, JP!" Ace and Connor were both dumbfounded while Avery and Daniella jumped up and down like a couple of giddy cheerleaders. Ace held his hands to his head in disbelief, saying, "Oh...my...God! Can that boy *drive*!"

Sean's helmet radio crackled. "Sean, do you think you can give JP a hand?" Billy Ray joked.

"Yeah, he looks kinda lonesome up there all by himself. Gimme ten laps, Billy. I think I can get this ride to move. It's getting loose on the right rear but I think I can handle it for now."

"Okay, Sean, we'll make an adjustment next time you're in for a pit stop."

Sean worked the car hard, increasing his lap time each time he went around the track, passing the remaining cars until he got to fourth place. Buzzy Durant, on the other hand, was losing ground fast as his tires were too worn to hold any speed. Sean just cruised by him, and it wasn't long before Buzzy lost air in his right front tire and went into a spin off the track and into the infield. Bits of rubber littered the track, and the caution flag came out. The pace car rolled out onto the track to slow the race to a safe speed as crews swept up the mess. Durant restarted his stalled car and managed to roll it around to pit road.

With less than fifty laps left in the race, everyone on pit road was busy calculating just what they needed to cross the finish line without any further stops. To save time in the pit and gain a tactical advantage, some crews opted to mount only two tires, while a few drivers merely stopped for gas, what they call "splash-n-go."

Billy Ray's biggest concern was his driver. Sean had to be in a lot of pain by now, but Billy Ray knew he was a tough kid. He figured if Sean's leg would hold up, he still had a chance to take the lead.

It would cost him more time in the pit, but Billy Ray gave orders for Sean to get four fresh tires and fuel. Sean was famous for pushing it to the limit. He drove himself hard, but he had the right car to do the job. The pit crew did what they had to do in lightening speed, and Sean got back on the track quickly.

The restart was a good one for Sean. He launched his car past Zimmer and was nose to nose with Dakota, who had the outside lane. Jimmy was behind Zimmer, looking for a way around him. A lot of the race cars were getting "marbles" or worn out rubber debris stuck in their tires on the outside lane. It would take a couple of laps before the tires were scrubbed free of the loose rubber and traction was restored.

Dakota and Sean were competing for the lead. She steered her car down in Sean's lane, giving him a bump sideways. It was an attempt at side-drafting, but Sean bumped her back, forcing her wheels to drive through some marbles. Sean started to pass when he saw Dakota's car begin to fishtail, bumping into the wall. Sean cut power to get clear of her, as she suddenly dove to the inside lane. This time Sean made sure she cleared his right front bumper and powered his way to the outside lane. Dakota struggled to stay on the track but lost traction and slid into the grass infield; she spun around and slid to a stop. She sped back onto the track but was well off the pace. Sean had the lead, but he lost his momentum dodging Dakota, and Carl Zimmer was coming up fast on the inside lane with Jimmy on the outside, almost even with him.

It was the last two laps of the race, and Jimmy came up fast on Sean's car, giving him a little push of momentum to keep ahead of Zimmer. The white flag was out, signaling the final lap. Sean switched to the inside lane, forcing Zimmer to let off the throttle slightly, just enough for Jimmy to get past Zimmer in the outside lane. The crowd was pushing up against the fence in front of the stands, yelling and cheering as Sean and Jimmy pulled away from Zimmer and the rest of the pack. The checkered flag was out. Sean's car roared past the stands in first place, with Jimmy taking second by only tenths of a second. Dakota did a valiant recovery, still managing to finish in the top ten.

Sean stopped in front of the stands at the finish line, where an official presented him with the checkered flag. He thought about doing a celebratory burn-out in front of the stands to please the fans, but his leg ached too much to manipulate the clutch pedal. Instead he paraded the car slowly, waving the checkered flag at the cheering fans. He turned around and pulled up to the finish line again, where he stopped the car.

The announcer said, "Folks, this year's Gator 500 winner, and three time PMRA champion: Sean Devlin!"

Sean leaned on his good leg for support as he waved the checkered flag triumphantly over his head, and then he bowed down to his adoring fans.

Sean climbed back into his car and revved the engine as he pulled away to victory lane. He stopped the car and climbed out more slowly since his knee was throbbing with more intensity and burning pain. Not even halfway out, he was already being sprayed by champagne. His family, his crew, and a crowd of supporters were cheering him, but his eyes only saw one person. "Daniella!" he yelled. "We won the Gator 500!"

She smiled brightly and shouted over the noise, "*You* won the Gator 500, my love!" And she kissed him.

A reporter nudged his way in with a microphone. "Sean...Sean Devlin, how do you feel?"

"Wonderful," he responded without any hesitation. Sean turned his head and beckoned to his brother Connor to join him. Sean threw his arm over Connor's shoulders and said, "This one is for you!"

Ace, Taylor, Avery, Sekou, Genji, Billy Ray, Dakota, and Hank all crowded around Sean, Daniella, and Connor. And standing there in the background were Benecio Villereal and Clayton. Jimmy wormed his way through the crowd to congratulate Sean. "Hey, buddy! Hellava race, huh?" he said as they shook hands.

Then another voice shouted, "Let's hear it for Jimmy Stanton!" And the press went wild with cameras, snapping picture after picture. Ace called out to Jimmy, "One more surprise, son!" Jimmy's father William Stanton III stepped out from behind Ace and ran up to his son, giving him a big hug. He said, "I'm so proud of you, son, and so is Ray Barber, who is right over there."

Jimmy waved to his former mentor and threw his arms around his father. "Dad! I can't believe you're here! I'm so happy to see you!"

Sean winked at his best friend and pointed at the trophy and mouthed, "The next one is yours, bro."

## CHAPTER NINETEEN
## *CELEBRATION*

After the ceremony on victory lane, the real celebrating began, complete with champagne being sprayed everywhere, and after the media blitz, Sean, Daniella, and his family headed over to his RV.

Ace and Taylor gave Sean and Daniella a big hug. However, Taylor pulled away just as Daniella leaned over to kiss her. "Oh, so sorry my dear, but my make-up, you know."

Daniella looked at Sean, who rolled his eyes and was about to say something to his mother when Ace interrupted, saying, *"Daniella*! You get *prettier* every day!" Then he gently took Taylor's arm and said, "Come, dear. Why don't we go and get something to drink?"

More guests arrived; the door swung open and Connor Devlin entered with his family in tow. Sean spotted them and hobbled over, whooping with happiness. He shouted to his sister-in-law, "Hi, Genji!" Before she could respond, he gave her a big kiss on her cheek. "It's been *too* long since we've seen each other!"

"Yes it has, Sean. Congratulations!" Genji said with a big smile.

Sean zeroed in on the infant Connor was cradling. "This must be my adorable, handsome nephew."

Genji took the baby from Connor and handed him to Sean, saying, "I now present to you Thomas 'Ace' Cho-Devlin!"

Sean reacted, "Aren't you cute?"

Hank yelled, "Wait, wait...Let me shoot some pictures. He's my nephew too!"

Avery, Sekou, Jimmy, Daniella, Ace, Taylor, and Clayton all crowded around Connor and Genji and the baby as Hank took several photos. Sean hugged and kissed his nephew, saying, "I love this kid!"

Hank, not being able to wait another minute to hold his nephew, scooped little Ace out of Sean's arms and smiled at the baby. "He's a fine boy, Genji! Connor, you must be very proud."

Connor grinned and put his arm around his wife.

Sean looked at all the faces at the party and smiled. He was surrounded by the most important people in his life, and even Jimmy was with his father.

Sean couldn't believe how great everything turned out. Jimmy was safe and sound, at least until his next screw-up. Sean thought to himself, *You can bet on that.*

Connor came forward, bearing a bit of good news from the track. He called for everyone to quiet down and said, "I have an announcement! Sean, listen! PMRA officials completed their initial investigation and they have rescinded Sean's bad post inspection, which had disqualified him from the Triax 400. Of course there are some other pending details, but Sean, thanks to Hank's help, it looks like you are in the clear!" Everybody cheered for Sean's good fortune.

It seemed like the beginning of a new chapter in the Devlin family.

## CHAPTER TWENTY
# SUDDEN DETOUR

Dakota Philips tugged at Billy Ray's sleeve and took him aside. "Baby, forgive me. I have a killer headache and I need to get out of here."

Billy Ray said, "Okay, let me take you home."

"No, no...I don't want to spoil your fun. You stay here and enjoy the rest of the Gator victory party. I'm tired after the race." She gave him a quick peck on the cheek good night and excused herself from the party after congratulating Sean. Dakota had a lot on her mind. For a brief moment she found herself torn between her loyalty to Billy Ray, Sean, and the DMS team and her ambition for *her* chance at victory lane.

Sometimes a little guilt would waft in and out of her quickly. A conscience was something she hadn't had in a long time, and forgot what it felt like. She had put up a protective shield long ago, so people and things would never get to her. She trained herself to not feel anything and had faked her emotions for most of her adult life.

It was getting late. Dakota was in a hurry to pack up her things before Billy Ray got home from the celebration. As she rushed about, trying to organize her packing, she bumped into a side table, which then toppled her backpack to the floor, spilling out a lot of her stuff, including her new cell phone and a few pieces of her mail.

She picked up the shiny new iPhone and looked at it for a moment. She thought about the man who gave it to her. Then she called him, and while waiting for a response, she continued packing, throwing all her clothes and things into her suitcase. Suddenly she heard his familiar craggy southern voice answer. She said, "Hi, Clayton. Are we still on for tonight?" She spoke to him in her most fake purr ever, even surprising herself. "Oh good, sugar," she said. "I've been missing you all day. Oh, don't worry about him. Billy's not going to be a problem anymore." She smiled to herself and knew she was right on track with her plan. "Okay," she said, "I'll meet you at your place in an hour. See you soon, lover." She hung up and tossed her phone in her bag.

Poor Billy Ray would be heartbroken. *Oh, he'll get over it*, she thought to herself as she threw her best negligee into her bag. Then she thought about all her friends at Devlin Motor Sports. *They will be really pissed*, she thought, *but all's fair in love and car racing!*

Everything was falling into place. *Ha!* She laughed to herself, thinking, *You ain't seen nothing yet, Mr. Clayton.* After all, it was she who had approached Clayton two months before, boldly declaring her aspirations of leaving Devlin Motor Sports for Villereal/Clayton Racing where she could become its next number one driver.

She picked up the envelope that was still lying on the floor; she noticed the name of a convent on the return address. "Oh yes," she said, "this must be about Billy's adoption. I'll read it later." She tossed the letter into her backpack. Billy Ray had asked her several months before to help find him information about his biological parents. Dakota, skilled in trolling the Internet, wound her way through the maze of adoption websites and found one that looked promising. Bluffing her way on the phone with just the right amount of tears and emotion, she was able to cajole an unsuspecting clerk into mailing her a copy of Billy Ray's birth certificate. Suddenly aware of the passing time, she looked at her watch and finished gathering her clothes.

She threw in one last item before closing her bag—the original flash drive that she had removed from Sean's car the night before the Triax 400. She remembered the thrill of sneaking into the DMS garage in the middle of the night and disabling the security wire that protected the car's flash drive, successfully removing it and replacing it with one that was programmed to make the car's on-board computer go out of control.

She was also the one who convinced Clayton to have Jimmy kidnapped from the Hotel Escondido. She knew that Sean and Jimmy would head to South Beach to blow off steam before the Triax. They were so predictable. When she saw them signing autographs, she planted a detection device under Sean's Corvette.

Clayton hired the thugs to play cards with Jimmy and set him up to lose for authenticity. With Jimmy missing in action and a no-show at the qualifying race, and Sean's chain reaction crash, it had put Devlin Motor Sports in a bad light. The Pro Motorsports Racing Association inspectors disqualified Sean from the Triax 400 after finding suspicious programming in his onboard computer. Eliminating the competition, Dakota won the Triax 400. She was feeling victorious, and there was no stopping her. But Sean raced in the Gator 500, and damn it, he *won*, even with an injured knee.

As she thought about all this and her plans to meet her new partner, she said, "Tsk tsk. Poor Clayton. You're putty in my hands."

## CHAPTER TWENTY-ONE
# KALEIDOSCOPE

Taylor Clayton Sr. stood at the bar in the corner of his library, deep in thought. His five mahogany trophy cases overflowed with many decades of car racing memorabilia. His library, like an elegant men's club, had the rich smell of leather, cigars, and fine scotch. The large oil painting of his deceased wife, Mariella, hung over the leather sofa. He reached for a fresh bottle of scotch and cracked it open. Pouring himself a drink, his mind continued to replay the day's events, which left a bad taste in his mouth. He had a hard time swallowing. It was a humiliating day for him at the race. Carl Zimmer was supposed to be a shoo-in to win the Gator 500. Villereal/Clayton Racing was supposed to bring home the coveted trophy.

"Damn it all! I'm surrounded by morons. I can't get anybody to do what they are told," he shouted in the empty room. Then he started laughing, thinking, *And Taylor's boy steals the race with a gimpy leg*. He laughed again, but eventually his face turned red as rage consumed him. "*Arrgh!*" He threw his glass at the wall and walked over to his desk with a wild look in his eyes.

He leaned on his desk and stared into space. He clenched his fist and pounded the desk. Images flashed in his intoxicated brain: the horrifying crash, his grandson's near death, the frightened look on Jimmy Stanton's face as he was tied up and pumped full of drugs. And now Ace was accusing him of trying to kill Taylor and that Billy Ray Harper kid. He suddenly felt exhausted; his body fell back into his desk chair.

"Old fool, you let yourself get caught up in too many webs," he said to himself. He got up to grab a fresh glass and poured himself another drink. Walking back to his desk, he said to himself, "You're a disgrace!" His self-loathing got worse the more he drank. "You have disgraced yourself and your family." He sat back down again; his bloodshot eyes were wet with tears. His hand shook as he leaned forward and opened the drawer that held a special key. The key unlocked a hidden compartment in his desk that held a loaded pistol.

He didn't feel the gun in his hand, and he didn't hear himself cock the hammer. His mind was playing and replaying all the horrible things he had done to his family. He regretted putting his grandson's life in danger, as well as his daughter's, and he regretted letting Dakota pressure him into a scheme to sabotage Sean's race car. How could he let anyone sway his better judgment? Yes, he was a lonely old man who welcomed the advances of an attractive young woman. Dakota caught him by surprise. She was so bright and persuasive. She reminded him of himself. Maybe that is why he let her get the best of him. She was so sexy; when she was with him, he couldn't think of anything else. He couldn't say no to her. He needed her. He focused on the gun in his hand. *I need her right now.* He thought about his son-in-law's words. *What am I going to do about Ace? He...*

But just then, Clayton's train of thought was interrupted. The sound of the intercom buzzer at the front gate broke the silence. His nerves still rattled by his son-in-law's threats, he reacted by shouting out, "Ace!" He looked around the room in heightened awareness when he heard the buzzer again. He uncocked the gun and placed it back in its secret compartment, locking the drawer. Pushing himself out of his chair, he finished the last drop of scotch in his glass and walked over to the intercom at the door. Pressing the button on the intercom, he barked, "Who is it?"

He heard Dakota's voice purr, "It's me, sugar."

"Oh...Dakota! Come in, girl!" He buzzed to open the gate for her and looked in a wall mirror, adjusting his collar and sweeping back his silvery hair with his hands. He looked like hell. Clayton practiced his best smile to cover up his misery.

Moments later, Dakota knocked on his door, and all of his previous misgivings melted away. His heart was already beating loudly in his chest. He opened the door and pulled her close, saying, "Get over here, girl. You don't know how happy I am to see you!"

With that, they both fell into each other's arms, kissing each other with intense passion. He became so excited he nearly dragged her to his bedroom. He hoped he wouldn't drop dead making love to her. At seventy-two years old, being in bed with Dakota made him feel young and powerful again—the way he used to be. If he could prolong his fantasy a little longer, why not—especially tonight.

When Clayton lost his young wife Mariella to cancer, his heart turned to stone. He never thought he would ever feel so strongly about someone again. So at that moment with Dakota, he was once more full of love and hope. He tried to memorize each and every second of their lovemaking and her lean athletic body, so he would always remember. His mouth on her perfect body, holding her lovely face, he would often reflect back to those royal-blue eyes that seemed to mask a lot of mystery and hidden pain. He knew he was not the love of her life, but he also knew that no one would ever be; he wondered what had caused such a young person to be so cold-hearted.

A little sex put Clayton in a better mood. He began thinking about tying up some loose ends he had with Dakota. After all, she was instrumental in sabotaging Sean's race car before the Triax 400. That girl was ruthless and would do anything to win. Clayton had to be prepared for future disappointment. He always had a back-up plan. Just in case Dakota betrayed him, he would need have some form of insurance to protect his interests.

He uncorked another bottle of wine and said, "Tell me what you think of this bottle." He smiled as he poured the wine into her glass.

After a few more glasses of wine, they chatted freely. He maneuvered the conversation to how she swapped flash drives in Sean's race car. She boasted about how she fooled everybody and how she lifted Billy Ray's keys when he was sleeping. Clayton asked, "What did you do with the original flash drive?"

She grinned and told him, "Oh, I still have that!"

Clayton pressed her, "You do? Where is it now?"

Taking another sip of wine, she said, "Oh, don't worry, it's safe. I have it in my bag." She smiled at him, enjoying her victory, and leaned over to him. "C'mon sugar." Grinding her body into his, she said, "What do you say...we talk...about something else."

He grabbed her and kissed her hard. "You're a wild cat! *Grrrouu!*" Clayton waited until she was in the shower after their lovemaking. He put on a pair of gloves and retrieved the flash drive from Dakota's bag, careful not to disturb the fingerprints. He placed the original #17 flash drive into a large envelope and wrote on it in bold letters: LIFE INSURANCE. He tore off a piece of paper from a pad and hurriedly wrote how Dakota Philips was responsible for Sean's Triax crash, Jimmy's kidnapping, and Sean's taser assault. Of course he left out any mention of his own involvement in the conspiracy. He sealed the envelope and climbed up the steep steps on his library ladder. Then he swung open a hinged oil painting that concealed the wall safe. After he opened the combination safe, Clayton put the envelope in with all of his other important papers. If Dakota stepped out of line, The Pro Motorsports Racing Association would mysteriously receive a #17 flash drive with Dakota's finger prints on it. PMRA would be forced to reopen the investigation and Dakota would take the fall. Clayton was so happy he had something to gloat about after a very trying day.

He went over to his desk and opened the center drawer to retrieve a duplicate flash drive. He made sure it was wiped clean of fingerprints. It looked just like the flash drive that belonged to Sean's car, complete with the #17 logo. Clayton planned to swap it for the *original* flash drive Dakota had in her bag.

As Clayton reached into her bag to plant the replacement, a letter slipped out and fell to the floor. In the background, he could hear Dakota calling to him from the shower. As he quickly bent over to retrieve the envelope, he began to feel dizzy. He couldn't quite get a hold of the thin edge of the envelope, fumbling try after try. "Damn these gloves!" He stood up and tore them off quickly and flung them into his leather waste paper basket. Clayton bent over again with a grunt and picked up the envelope. Just as he was about to slip it back into her bag, his curiosity got to him and he turned it face up and glimpsed at the return address. Recognizing it immediately, his face froze into a mask of terror. *What could Dakota be doing with a letter from* this *convent?* he thought. *If this is what I think it is, then I'll be ruined, along with a lot of other people.* He saw that the letter was still sealed. *Good! At least she hadn't read it.* He tore open the letter and found two documents. He whispered aloud, "Oh God!" He realized that all hell would break loose if anyone read the explosive information in the papers.

Enclosed was a copy of a birth certificate of the baby boy of Rosalinda Celestina and Benecio Villereal, along with a second document showing the baby had been adopted by Michael and Ann Harper. Clayton's chest tightened. It was Billy Ray's adoption papers. He was reeling from the shocking revelation that his partner, Benecio Villereal, was Billy Ray Harper's biological father. *It had to be true*, he thought. *Rosalinda's baby was adopted by the Harpers.* He thought about Billy Ray's looks. He resembled Villereal. Even his age at thirty was in the right ball park. *One of these days, I am going to have to tell Benecio that Billy Ray is his son.*

Clayton was having difficulty breathing. He had to move fast to lock up the letter so no one would ever find it. His heart was pounding very quickly in an unfamiliar way. He struggled to get to his desk as quickly as he could and find his special drawer. His hands began to shake. He put the letter inside the hidden drawer that also held his gun, locked it up, and hid the key inside a secret compartment he had custom made for his desk. It was getting harder and harder for him to breathe, but he knew he had to move away from the desk to throw off any suspicions Dakota might have if she caught him standing there.

He was struggling to walk away and maintain his balance when he began to choke uncontrollably. Then he couldn't breathe at all. His face was turning blue. Clutching his heart in agony, he cried out, "Oh...my God!" and he collapsed to the floor.

Clayton was out cold on the carpet. Snapshots of his life in Goldsboro, North Carolina from thirty years ago, came flooding into view like a kid's kaleidoscope. His beautiful seventeen year old daughter

Taylor, was spoiled and headstrong. Clayton hired a maid, Bonita, to take care of her. By then Taylor had fallen deeply in love with a very handsome young man named Benecio Villereal, also seventeen, the son of his Mexican business partner, Felipe Villereal. Clayton and Felipe co-owned the VL Clayton Tobacco Company. Benecio and Taylor became inseparable, he with his striking good looks and she a tall icy beauty, with blonde hair and blue eyes. Sometimes Bonita would bring along her eighteen-year-old niece, Rosalinda Celestina, who was living with Bonita and her family. Rosalinda, beautiful and fiery, also caught young Benecio's eye. The two of them would often sneak away without anyone knowing.

One day, Clayton happened to catch Taylor glancing out of his office window and as he looked out himself he saw what she saw, that of Benecio embracing Rosalinda. Clayton knew his daughter would be crushed. Her world fell apart. He also knew that somehow Taylor would seek revenge on Rosalinda. Taylor never spoke about it to anyone, not even to her lover, Benecio, or to her father.

Taylor was raised as a tomboy, and she became skilled in many sports, including Clayton's other business, car racing. Driving fast cars was her favorite sport, and it drew her closer to her father since she was more like a son than her older brother, Edward. He was a colossal embarrassment to his father because he was fat and lazy, and not into sports at all. All he wanted to do was read and go to school. Taylor gladly stepped into his shoes by excelling in anything she was interested in and became a very talented race car driver—fearless. She was taught to race by her father and by some of the other top drivers around.

Taylor planned to lure Rosalinda away from the house on the pretext of going shopping. Then once Rosalinda was alone with her, she would confront her about her relationship with Benecio and scare her into breaking it off with him.

The kaleidoscope turned again. Before Taylor could carry out her plan, Rosalinda found herself pregnant with Benecio Villereal's baby. Being a good Catholic girl, she felt disgraced and was unable to tell her Aunt Bonita or her lover, Benecio; she went to Clayton and pleaded for his help. Feeling sorry for the girl and sorrier for his daughter, if she were to find out, Clayton arranged for Rosalinda to go to Sisters of the Blessed Mother Convent, hundreds of miles away. She would live there and go to school until it was time for her to give birth. Once the baby was born, Sister Esperanza would put the baby up for adoption. Clayton told Rosalinda she would be able to return home to her Aunt Bonita about ten months after everything had been properly taken care of. He swore Rosalinda to secrecy and extracted a promise that she would not contact Benecio. Clayton made a very large donation to the convent on behalf of his gratitude for their acts of charity. The story he told her family was that Rosalinda has been diagnosed with a rare type of lung disease and had to be sent to a sanitarium that specialized in that illness. Although it was far away, she had to stay there until she was fully cured. He even had his family doctor confirm the story.

The family doctor kept Clayton informed of Rosalinda's progress. He was rewarded handsomely for his discretion. Taylor and Benecio never found out about the baby. Benecio, although missing Rosalinda a great deal, resumed his love affair with Taylor.

The ten months passed quickly, and one day Bonita showed up with Rosalinda supposedly all healthy and cured. She was even lovelier. Clayton knew how jealous Taylor was of Rosalinda and observed his daughter's reactions. Everyone greeted Rosalinda warmly, except Taylor. It was obvious that Rosalinda still had feelings for Benecio no matter how hard she tried to conceal them, and by the way Benecio fawned all over her, it was clear that he still felt very strongly about her as well. Clayton could tell by the look on his daughter's face that she was going to take it out on Rosalinda in some way.

Taylor, greeted Rosalinda with: "Welcome back, Rosalinda. I'd like to celebrate your homecoming by treating you to a day of shopping. Okay?"

"Yes, Ms. Taylor," said Rosalinda. "That would be fun."

The two girls made their plans and the next day they took off on their shopping date in Clayton's sports car with Taylor driving. They didn't tell anyone so they wouldn't have to keep to a schedule.

What happened next was a mystery to Clayton and to everyone who was at the scene that day. After all these years, Clayton had asked himself how it could have happened. What really happened? He played it over in his mind hundreds of times. Knowing his daughter so well, and putting the pieces together after talking to the traffic police, he figured this was the logical scenario:

Already speeding, Taylor wanted to scare the hell out of Rosalinda and then confront her about her true feelings for Benecio. Suddenly, a large truck pulled out in front of them. Taylor tried to pass the truck and pulled out into the oncoming traffic. With such a fast car, she was sure she had time to speed up and pass in front of the truck, when out of nowhere a car came hurtling toward them. Taylor violently swerved the car and miraculously avoided crashing headlong into the oncoming car, but her car flew off the road, just before smashing into a tree.

Both girls were ejected from the car. Rosalinda's body hit the tree with such a deadly impact that she was killed instantly. Taylor was thrown clear to the side of the road, miraculously landing on some brush that spared her life. When the ambulance and police arrived, Taylor, though in shock, had them call her father. She never looked at Rosalinda's dead body.

Clayton paid everyone off to expunge any record of the accident. Thus, his daughter Taylor's life was spared a second time, and he made sure that she would never be charged with vehicular manslaughter.

The driver of the oncoming car was never heard from again. His daughter never spoke of what happened, and neither did he. Their family doctor reassured him that in such cases of extreme trauma, it was almost definite that her memory about the horrific crash would be permanently wiped clean.

Benecio and everyone else heard about the tragic news of Rosalinda's death on television; that she had been struck and killed by a hit-and-run driver while crossing the street. The driver of the car was never found. That fictitious story had been planted by Clayton to divert the truth—that his daughter Taylor was responsible for Rosalinda's death.

Clayton heard from Bonita that Benecio quietly grieved for Rosalinda and confessed to her that he had truly loved Rosalinda and would have asked her to marry him.

As Clayton lay on the floor, semiconscious, the shock of seeing the return address on a letter that had spilled out of Dakota's bag from the Sisters of the Blessed Mother, the convent where he had sent Rosalinda so very long ago, had triggered a terrible feeling deep within his soul; that somehow this would all come back to haunt him.

Dakota had finished her shower and called out to Clayton as she was toweling off, "Hey sugar, I was just think..." She peeked her head out of the bathroom doorway and realized he wasn't in the bedroom anymore. She wandered out into the living room. Not finding him there, she went into his library, calling out, "Where are you, sugar? Hey sugar?" She found him lying on the rug. "Clayton?" she cried. "Can you hear me? Clayton, you're scaring me. Wake up!" She leaned over and checked to see if he was breathing. Then she checked his pulse. "Come on, Clayton. Damn it, wake up! Clayton! Clayton!" She couldn't lose him. "This can't be happening." She pulled out her iPhone and dialed 911 for help. As she dialed, she said, "Clayton, don't you do this to me, damn it to hell! Clayton! Wake up!" Rattled and panicked, she ran back to the bedroom to get dressed.

Waiting for the ambulance to arrive, a million thoughts went through her head. Suddenly, her plans were in jeopardy, and she weighed her options. She looked at Clayton on the floor and thought, *Crap! What if something happens to him? All my plans...a total waste.* She pursed her lips and considered, *Well, I could always go back to DMS if Clayton doesn't make it.*

## CHAPTER TWENTY-TWO
# *HEARTACHE*

T he phone at the Devlin Ormond Beach condo broke the calm silence of the night. In the darkness, Taylor fumbled for the lamp
on her bedside table. Still half asleep, she answered the phone. "Hullo?
What? Who is this? My father's in the hospital? What happened...Is he
all right?" She listened for a moment and answered, "Yes, we're on our
way," and hung up the phone. "Ace!" She nudged her husband. "Ace,
wake up. Daddy's in the hospital. They think he's had a stroke."

Ace stirred out of his sleep. "What, honey?"

"Get dressed! We got to go to the hospital!"

Ace pulled back the blankets to get up as he began to think aloud.
"I better wake Connor, and I'll have him call Sean from the car. Oh my
God, it's two in the morning. Why do these things always happen in
the middle of the night?"

Taylor, rushing to pull on some clothes, barked, "Come on, Ace!
Get a move on! And don't wake the baby and Genji. We'll call everyone else later."

The brightly lit hospital parking lot was nearly empty when Ace
drove in with Taylor and Connor. They all raced to the emergency
room entrance, with Taylor leading the way. She dashed over to the
registration desk and announced. "I'm Taylor Devlin. You have my
father here."

The nurse said, "What's his name?"

"Taylor Clayton Sr."

"Oh yes, Ms. Devlin, the doctor is with him now. I'll let him know you are here."

"Who brought him in?"

"He came by ambulance. A dark haired girl was with him."

Taylor looked puzzled. "Who?"

The door swung open, and a girl holding a cup of coffee walked into the waiting room. The nurse spotted her and pointed over Taylor's shoulder, "That girl."

Taylor turned her head just as she heard Ace say, "Dakota! What are you doing here? Is Billy Ray here too?"

Taylor stared at Dakota, studying her every feature and every move. Full of anger and suspicion, she marched across the waiting room, shoving Ace aside. "All right missy, what the hell's going on?"

Dakota stared right back at Taylor; she looked directly into her eyes and said, "Mrs. Devlin, I brought your father here because he seemed to have suffered a stroke. If it weren't for me, he'd probably be dead."

Taylor confronted Dakota again. "What were you doin' with my father so late at night?"

Dakota coolly responded, "Clayton and I are very good friends, Mrs. Devlin. We were just having a drink together when he became seriously ill. Look, Mrs. Devlin, my relationship with Clayton is really none of your business. I would think you'd be more in a rush to talk to Clayton's doctor rather than interrogating me!"

Ace tried to stop Taylor, but it was too late as she hauled off and slapped Dakota hard across her face. Dakota's coffee spilled all over her shoes and the floor, making a mess. Taylor looked at Dakota and asked, "What do you mean, you and my daddy are good friends?"

Ace pulled on Taylor's shoulder and said, "All right, enough of this! We are all here for Clayton. Let's focus our attention on him. Connor, see if you can find his doctor. Somebody needs to tell us what's going on. Taylor, come sit down with me. Dakota, it looks like you and I have a few things to straighten out. We'll talk in the morning."

Dakota rubbed the welt on her face. "Right, boss. We need to talk."

A young doctor held the door to the emergency room. "Mrs. Devlin, will you come this way?"

Taylor turned to Ace. Tears welling up in her eyes. She grabbed hold of his hand. "Ace, come with me."

He hugged her. "Of course, deah." They followed the doctor into the emergency room.

Dakota, badly shaken and freaked out over her confrontation with Taylor, decided to go home to see Billy Ray. Maybe she could sweet talk her way back in with him since her future with Clayton seemed very uncertain. She'd have to revise her plan of action, and her top priority would be to find a new place to live in case she couldn't smooth things over with Billy Ray. *As long as Clayton keeps his mouth shut, I shouldn't have any problem keeping my job at DMS*, she thought. *I know how to handle Ace.*

She saw Sean pulling into the hospital's parking lot and quickly ducked around the back to avoid any more surprise reactions from any of the Devlins. She waited a few minutes, and when the coast was clear, she walked over to a phone at the entrance of the hospital and called for a cab. It came quickly, and she gave the driver Billy Ray's address, her old address. The cab drove away.

Dr. Schottstein was greeting the Devlins when, Sean came limping over. The doctor, seeing Sean, wagged his finger at him and said, "I thought I told you to stay off that leg for a while," winking at him, as he ushered them all into an office to talk. Having been their Ormond Beach doctor for a long time, he tried to present Clayton's serious prognosis in a gentle way. "Let me begin by saying your father is comfortable and we're doing everything possible to stabilize him. He suffered a severe stroke."

Taylor gasped and began to sob. Ace, Sean, and Connor all looked at each other and then at Taylor in shock. Ace, gripping Taylor's hand tightly, leaned over and kissed her, saying, "There, there, my deah. We'll do whatever it takes."

Dr. Schottstein continued, "In these cases, the first forty-eight hours are the most critical. But your father has some good things going for him. Fortunately, he received help immediately. I'd be beholden to that young lady who called the ambulance right away."

Sean said, "Who was that?"

Connor answered, "Dakota Philips. I'll explain later." Sean looked at his brother, puzzled.

"He has paralysis on the right side of his body and he can't speak at the moment, but he can think clearly. We are hopeful. If your father rallies in the next few days, the plan will be to send him to our rehabilitation facility for intensive therapy to get him walking and eventually talking."

Taylor threw her arms around Ace and sobbed, "Oh, Daddy...poor Daddy! What did he do to deserve this?" Ace held his wife and stared off into the distance, lost in his thoughts.

**DAKOTA'S CAB PULLED** up outside Billy Ray's RV. Dakota asked the driver, "Would you please wait a few minutes until I come back?"

"Sure, ma'am, I'll wait. I know who you are; you're that lady racing driver."

She walked toward the RV. She felt very awkward knocking on their door at four in the morning but gave a few good raps on it with her knuckles anyway. After a bit, the lights went on inside and a sleepy Billy Ray peered out and saw her.

He opened the door and said, "You're the last person I ever expected to see. You forget somethin'?"

Dakota said, "Billy, I..."

Billy Ray didn't want to hear it. He turned his head away, annoyed, and interrupted her, "What the hell are you doing here? I thought you left me for good."

Dakota begged, with a pleading look on her face, "Please Billy, I need to talk to you. Please! It's just awful. Everyth..."

He said, "It's too late, Dakota. I begged you time after time to talk, and you never gave me a chance. So I'm returning the favor. It's *over*!"

He slammed the door shut. She stood there in the dark, stunned.

She climbed back into the waiting taxi and just sat in silence. The driver finally said, "Where to, ma'am?"

She said, "Please, I need a minute," and began running her fingers through her long black hair, trying to think. She rummaged through her bag and fished out some keys. *Ahh, right,* she thought. *My car's still parked at Clayton's, and I have his house keys. I might as well stay the night.*

After giving the cab driver Clayton's address, Dakota leaned back in the seat and closed her eyes.

## CHAPTER TWENTY-THREE
# *SWITCHING GEARS*

D akota Philips let herself into Clayton's condo. It was around five in the morning. Her shoes smelled of coffee and they were ruined. Her cheek was still throbbing from when Taylor hauled off and socked her. What a scene with Taylor. She would have to square everything with Ace. Her acting would come in handy. She knew that Taylor wouldn't let her stay at Clayton's house, so she'd have to find a new place to live immediately. It was all over with Billy Ray. She couldn't believe he didn't take her back. She thought, *My life is falling apart.* Too exhausted and overwhelmed to think clearly, she wandered down the long hallway to Clayton's guest room, tumbled into the bed, and tried to fall asleep, but her head was filled with the terrible jarring events that had taken place a few hours before. Clayton's stroke and Billy Ray's all-out rejection of her had shaken her to the core. After suppressing her childhood memories for so many years, she now wished she could summon up her beloved grandfather Slim, who was always there to soothe her hurting soul.

When she was growing up in Goldsboro, North Carolina, her parents were never around, so her grandparents Lila and Slim looked after her. Her father, Blake Philips, an engineer, seemed to lose jobs as quickly as he got them, and her mom, Clarissa Turner Philips, a trained architect, would go off with him. They had been childhood sweethearts and still remained inseparable. "They shouldn't have had any children," she remembered Grandpa Slim saying once "Free spirits—that's what they've always been."

One day when everyone was home, Dakota heard a terrible commotion—a lot of screaming and crying. She ran into her parents' bedroom and there was her mother, hysterical, and holding the lifeless body of her baby brother Daniel in her arms. Dakota watched in shock as her mother rocked back and forth, her sobs of grief made Dakota's ears ring. Daniel's long, dark curls blew around his still face, as if somehow the movement would wake him up and he'd come back to life.

Dakota collapsed on the floor and was breathing funny. Her Grandpa Slim tried to get her to breathe into a paper bag. The rest of the day was a complete fog of memories, with strange people who traipsed in and out of the house. Once she thought she saw some stranger carry out her baby brother's little body wrapped in his blue velvet blanket. It was all too much for her. From that awful day on, she made a vow that she would never let herself get too close to another person. Ever! She wouldn't subject herself to that unbearable pain again. All Dakota wanted to do was go and join Daniel in his grave. The thought of her beloved little brother being buried under all that dirt, all alone and cold, was too much for her young mind to grasp. The doctor said Daniel died from Sudden Infant Death Syndrome. No one knew what that was back then. They called it "crib death." It was some sort of mysterious illness that killed many babies without any real reason.

Not long after that tragic day, Dakota's parents took off and never returned. The rest of her family tried to heal and carry on. Late one night, about a year after they left, Grandpa Slim got a call from a policeman in Taylors, South Carolina. He identified himself as Officer Hampton and informed her grandfather that her parents had died in a terrible accident. Dakota could overhear his high-pitched, nasally voice, even from ten feet away. She listened to him tell her grandpa the gruesome details of how they died. They had been riding on her dad's Harley, his favorite motorcycle, the one she remembered he painted the blue and green dragons on. Officer Hampton said it looked like they had been travelling about 90 miles an hour in a 45 mile an hour zone. Somehow, her father must have lost control of the motorcycle, and it crashed through a guardrail and plunged down a ravine. The police found her mother and father in the ravine near each other, with her mother's arms stretched out toward her father. The policeman said they probably died instantly, as if the family might find any comfort in that. He also added that it might have been from too much drugs and alcohol, but everyone knew it was from their broken hearts. Grandpa Slim had their bodies flown home to Goldsboro, so they could be buried in the family plot next to her baby brother, Daniel. Her baby brother wouldn't have to be all alone anymore.

Once again, Slim, Lila, and Dakota had to heal and carry on. Her heart was just getting heavier and heavier from the weight of her grief.

Dakota was always reading books. There seemed to be a never-ending supply of new books to read on her nightstand, which distracted her from her sadness. Grandpa Slim told people that Dakota was wise beyond her years. He tried to help her get over all of the deaths by taking her on nightly walks around town. He liked to stop by the same big house in the fancy part of town called, "Golden Springs," and he would point out, "See, Dakota, that big house belongs to Taylor Clayton Sr. He makes his money from growing tobacco. See that track? That's where he has his racing teams practice."

Grandpa Slim introduced Dakota to a whole new world, which helped erase the terrible one she was living in. He taught her about stock car racing and would explain to her in detail what was happening as the racers were driving around the track. Dakota became fascinated with speed and soon began to fantasize about having a life in racing. She just knew that this was what she wanted to do more than anything else. Grandpa Slim helped prepare her for such a life, and he was the one who some time later got her first job as a mechanic at his friend Burdie Graham's garage. Grandpa Slim was a great mechanic too, and everyone in Goldsboro and beyond knew about Slim's Fix-It Garage.

Dakota watched and learned. Her sharp mind soaked up every detail. She used to say, "I'm going to be somebody, Grandpa, and I'm going to end up in a big house just like that rich man Clayton."

A noise in the condo woke Dakota up. She sat up in bed and listened and decided to go take a look.

## CHAPTER TWENTY-FOUR
## *REVELATIONS*

T aylor Devlin used her spare key to get into her father's Ormond Beach condo. Earlier, she had watched her father Clayton struggle to communicate with her as he lay in his hospital bed. His massive stroke rendered him, at least temporarily, incapable of speech, and he was paralyzed on his right side. It had broken her heart to see her beloved father in such fragile health. Clayton used hand gestures and finger tapping with his good left hand, to let her know how urgent it was for her to go to his condo in Ormond Beach and retrieve some of his important documents. She suspected that her father was afraid he might die in the hospital and wanted her to have them.

First up on her father's list was his wall safe that was located in his library. She climbed up the tall ladder. She swung aside the hinged oil painting to reveal the safe. She reached into her pocket and pulled out the piece of paper that had the safe's combination that Clayton had somehow tapped out for her. Taylor's hand shook as she spun the dial and waited for the tumblers to fall into place. Within seconds, the safe opened.

She found the envelope that was labeled LIFE INSURANCE written in her father's scribbled handwriting. Confused when she realized it wasn't an insurance policy, Taylor found a note inside written in Clayton's scrawl. It explained that he had taken the original #17 flash drive from Dakota Philips, the one she had removed from Sean's racing car right before the Triax 400. Further, it detailed how Dakota

120

knowingly planted a defective flash drive in Sean's car, which ultimately caused the crash that nearly killed him and lastly, Dakota was the mastermind behind the plan to kidnap Jimmy Stanton.

Taylor's blood boiled. Shaking with such rage she screamed out, "I'm gonna kill her!" She took her father's envelope, and instead of putting it back into his safe, she decided to take it with her and keep it in her own private safe until he was well enough to go home and then she'd return it. At that time, she would have a discussion with him about why he had kept such dark, ugly secrets. If he knew about that secret, what else did he know?

She closed the safe and put everything back in order and climbed down. She placed the envelope in her purse.

The next place her father wanted her to check on was his antique, carved, wooden desk. She unhooked the keys from their special hiding place under one of the desk drawers. Her father had a desk exactly like this one when they were growing up in North Carolina, so she knew all of the tricks. She jimmied a drawer that looked out of place. Taylor jiggled it around some more until it popped open. She found a letter on top and her curiosity forced her to look at the return address. She read it aloud to herself, "The Sisters of the Blessed Mother Convent, Slatesville, North Carolina. Hmm, what's this?"

She opened the envelope. There were two documents inside. Taylor removed one and quickly read it. It was a birth certificate that stated on June 15, 1984, Rosalinda Celestina had given birth to a baby boy and that the birth father's name was Benecio Villereal. Taylor was in shock! Shaking uncontrollably she screamed out, "No! This can't be! Benecio was *my* boyfriend. We were still lovers, and we were both only 17 years old. I can't believe he deceived me and knocked up that girl. I could kill him I am so furious!"

The other document stated that the baby boy was adopted by Michael and Anne Harper. "What is this?" she yelled. Our Billy Ray Harper is Benecio's son?" Overwhelmed, Taylor caught herself just as she fell back into the desk chair, hitting her head on the edge of the hanging wooden book shelf on her way down.

The list of people Taylor wanted to kill had grown, but Dakota was definitely right up there. "I am going to kick her ass when I see her."

Taylor paused and looked up. She thought she heard a noise that came from a back room in Clayton's condo. She shoved the rest of the papers into her purse and silently crept out of the library. She walked slowly toward the noise. When she turned the corner that led to the guest bedroom, she practically slammed right into Dakota Philips. Her rage at the sight of Dakota overcame her. Taylor screamed, "What the hell are you still doing here? I could kill you right now for breaking and entering, then call it self-defense. My son, Sean, almost died because of you, you evil bitch!"

Before Dakota had a chance to defend herself, Taylor smashed her fist into Dakota's face. Dakota crumpled to the floor, unconscious. Her body ceased to move as blood oozed from her nose. Taylor couldn't resist and kicked Dakota hard in the ribs.

## CHAPTER TWENTY-FIVE
# *THREE'S A CROWD*

A ce woke up and realized Taylor hadn't come back from Clayton's condo. It was 2:30 a.m., and he was starting to worry. He called her cell phone. No answer. "Oh come on, Taylor! Why aren't you picking up?" He knew she had to sort through a lot of Clayton's things: mail, personal papers, and more of his clothes.

He called her again and then he heard her voice. "Oh Ace, I banged my head really hard on one of the book shelves."

"Are you all right, deah? I have been so worried. I was just going to go to Clayton's and check up on you."

"Well, I was going to..."

"Honey don't do anything. I'll be right there. Stay put, deah. If your dad has any ice, put some on your head now." Then he joked, "Honestly, the hospital should give us a special group rate the way our family has been filling their beds lately."

Impatient at what she was holding in her hand, Taylor said, "Honee, you won't believe what I found in Daddy's safe and desk! I can't wait for you to get here! Hurry!"

"Okay, deah, I'm on my way.

**TAYLOR HEARD ACE'S** car pull up to the front of her father's condo. She buzzed him in. He hugged her close and kissed her head.

"Oh deah, how's your head?" he said to her as he studied her for injuries. She waved him away and told him to follow her down the hallway. There, sitting on the tiled floor propped up against the wall, was Dakota. Her face was all bloody and battered. Her hands were tied up with some kind of cable wire.

Ace asked, "What the blazes happened heah?"

Taylor blurted out, "Ace, I found something in Daddy's papers that proves Sean's crash was no accident. And furthermore, I know who sabotaged Sean's car, and I have the evidence!"

She reached into her handbag and pulled out the envelope she found in her father's safe. Holding the envelope in front of Ace's face, she angrily yelled, "Here look inside this envelope!"

Ace reached into the envelope and pulled out a PMRA flash drive labeled "#17."

Ace stared at the flash drive.

Taylor continued to shout, "You know what, Ace? It was Dakota who switched out that flash drive from Sean's car and replaced it with a defective one that caused Sean's car to crash! Daddy wrote a note saying so!" Taylor stared into Ace's eyes and continued shouting, "And not only that, Daddy says in the note that *she* was the one who planned Jimmy's kidnapping!"

Taylor planted her hands on her hips and said, "And do you know I'm sure that bitch seduced my father and manipulated him?"

Ace pointed to Dakota and said, "But Taylor, how could you...?" Then he shook his head in disbelief. "Cooler heads must prevail. I realize you wanted to kill her and so do I, but you didn't have to hit her so hard." He knelt down to examine Dakota's injuries.

He gently picked up her swollen chin and looked into her eyes as they fluttered open and then closed. "Oh my God, Taylor! You really hurt her! She's barely conscious. I never knew you were capable of such violence!"

Dakota moaned a little. Ace carefully untied the cable wire that Taylor had used to bind her wrists. It had left deep red ridges. "I'll have to think of something fast if the paramedics ask about those marks, he said. He went to hide the wire.

Right after Ace called 911, he turned to Taylor and said, "I hope her nose isn't broken! Taylor, quick, go get some ice for her face. We'll say it was very dark when you came into the house, and you thought she was an intruder, so you hit her."

Taylor interrupted him and said, "Ace, I have one more thing to show you..." She reached into her handbag to get Billy Ray's birth certificate.

## CHAPTER TWENTY-SIX
## *PIT STOP*

D akota awoke and immediately knew she was in the hospital. She vaguely remembered hearing the paramedics in the ambulance saying something about her being severely beaten. It was Taylor who beat her, that part she remembered.

The sounds, the smells in the hospital were all too familiar to her; remembering back to when she had had all of her reconstructive surgeries. She felt awful. She thought, *Thank God that crazy, homicidal maniac Taylor didn't break my nose or any of my bones.* But Dakota's face still hurt like hell, and her ribs were still very sore and tender. *She's a vile, evil, demonic woman!* The doctor told her she'd fully recover but it would take some time for her injuries to heal.

Dakota dozed off after she was given her pain meds. Something made her look up, and she saw Ace Devlin standing over her bed. *Holy crap!* He looked very serious and said, "How are you feeling, Dakota?"

*I better keep my mouth shut,* she thought, *before I let him know how pissed off I am about what his crazy bitch wife did to me, but he's my boss.* "Well boss, not so great. But I'll be fine for Dover."

"Dakota, we have to talk. I feel terrible about what happened to you, really. But under the circumstances with your tampering of Sean's flash drive, I'm going to have to let you go. You're fired."

"But boss!"

"I could have you arrested," Ace said sternly, "and you must know why Taylor wanted you dead. You haven't even shown any remorse for what you did to Sean and to us. I don't know where we went wrong. We all believed in you. You cold bloodedly rigged it so my son's car would crash, and damn it to hell, Sean almost died in that crash! You should have been arrested for attempted murder." Ace leaned forward and said, "This is what's going to happen Dakota: You will no longer drive for DMS. *That's* a given. Taylor is going to race in your place. I spoke to Benecio Villereal, and he's willing to let you drive for Villereal/Clayton. I am very sorry you were so badly beaten, and quite frankly, I was very surprised my wife would do such a thing. But we're willing to move on, and I suggest you do, too."

Ace walked out.

Dakota thought, *I'll be driving for the Villereal/Clayton Racing team and Taylor will be racing in my place for DMS. I have three weeks to heal before the Dover race. I'm going to have to whup that bitch's ass and win.*

As Ace was leaving, he bumped into his brother-in-law Edward Clayton, in the hallway. Edward had just arrived from New York City to see Dakota. Ace had called Edward earlier and told him about Dakota's beating and suggested he fly right down to Ormond Beach. They chatted, and Ace briefed him on the latest trouble Dakota was in including the sad fact that he had just fired her.

Ace had been friends with Edward, his wife Taylor's brother, for years, going back to when Edward, fresh out of college asked Ace for a job. Ace had just opened up Devlin Media in New York City, and set Edward up in his own publishing company, EMP (Edward Mariella Publishing.) It was now a leading publisher of art and design books. He and Ace said their goodbyes and Edward knocked on Dakota's door before letting himself in.

Edward greeted her with a smile and Dakota was thrilled to see her good friend—actually, her only friend. She tried to get up to greet him, but her bruised ribs prevented her from moving. Edward looked at all of her injuries.

"Well, my dear girl, how are you doing?" Edward leaned over her bed and kissed her on the cheek. "Heard you got yourself into some hot water."

"I'm hanging in there," she said. "I guess everything in my life is falling apart, Edward."

"Now, now, Dakota. You have a job racing for Benecio's team, and I'm here to help you recover. Isn't that good? And hey, Dakota, you're not in jail yet. I'd say you're doing okay. But, your blind ambition will be your downfall. I am going to have to retain a lawyer for you. We have to have a serious talk about your obsession with winning. What I can't believe is that you haven't shown any remorse for being responsible for my nephew Sean's, near fatal crash. You did it just so you could win a race. I don't know you anymore, Dakota. I think you have ice in your veins!"

"Edward, I'm so glad you're here," she said, trying to change the topic.

Still groggy from her pain medicine, her head fell back on the pillow, and she closed her eyes. Edward took that as his cue to go and get a cup of coffee.

As she drifted in and out of sleep, she remembered back to that fateful night when she and Edward first met and how their lives literally collided.

Dakota was only sixteen years old at the time. She had taken her grandfather Slim's favorite car, a red Mustang, out for a joyride. As she raced through the streets of Goldsboro, Dakota imagined she was one of those race car drivers at that rich man's track.

Speeding into an intersection, she barreled through a red light and was suddenly blindsided on the Mustang's passenger side by a car rushing into the intersection. The impact was so great, that as the Mustang flipped over a few times, Dakota's body sailed through the back window, spraying shattered glass everywhere. She landed on the side of the road, all bloody and broken.

All she remembered about that night was being wrapped in bandages like a mummy and racked with the most horrific pain. She heard a man's voice but didn't recognize it. He told her he was Edward Clayton. *Edward?* His name was somehow familiar to her, but in her nearly unconscious haze, it was just a name. The next few weeks, Edward Clayton was her most frequent visitor, besides her grandparents.

Before the accident, she was okay looking but not that attractive. She had her father's tall, athletic, lean build and her mother's dark blue eyes and long black silky hair. Dakota didn't care what she looked like since she was a tomboy and only hung out with the mechanics who worked for Slim and some of the local boys from school.

As Dakota lay in her hospital bed recovering from her awful car crash, she asked Edward if he would tell her his side of what happened the night of their accident.

Edward agreed and in a way, he felt slightly responsible. He had been drinking heavily, and was on his way to a friend's house. He approached the intersection and as the light turned green, he stomped on the accelerator. Suddenly, Edward saw a blur of red hurtling through the intersection. And then, *CRASH*, the front of his car plowed into the passenger side of the red Mustang. He watched as the other car went hurtling off the road and landed in a ditch. His own car, a Pontiac GTO, was badly crushed in the front, but by some miracle, Edward had been able to walk away with just some minor cuts and bruises.

Edward ran over to the young girl lying on the ground, bloody and unconscious.

He then hurried over to the wrecked Mustang to see if he could find her contact information. He grabbed what papers he could find out of the partially intact glove compartment and stuffed them into his pocket. Edward knew he had to get help fast.

Edward spotted a phone booth on the corner, and raced over to it, and called for an ambulance. It arrived quickly and they were both transported to the Goldsboro Hospital Trauma Center, a few miles away.

The next part of the story Edward completely left out and did not tell Dakota: After he was treated for his minor injuries and released, Edward found a public phone in the hospital and called his father, Clayton Sr. and told him about the terrible car crash he had just been involved in with a young girl, who was severely injured. Edward briefed him in on all of the pertinent details and asked his father to handle the police and to take care of everything else. His father was a master at protecting the family name. Edward told his father that he himself would be responsible for all of the girl's medical bills.

Then, Edward pulled out the papers he retrieved from the Mustang, and dialed the contact phone number. The man who answered, identified himself as Slim Philips, the same name that appeared on the car's registration. When Edward identified himself, Slim recognized the Clayton name.

Edward asked the man if he knew the young girl who was driving his Mustang. There was a pause in the conversation. A minute later, Slim got back on the line and told Edward his Mustang was missing and that his granddaughter Dakota must have taken it. He demanded to know what was going on. First, with some coaxing from Edward, Slim gave him a physical description of his granddaughter, to see if it matched the girl from the accident. It did match. Edward told Slim about their crash, and explained that it had happened so quickly, he didn't have a chance to swerve out of the way. His granddaughter had come barreling out of nowhere like a bat out of hell. Edward told Slim that his granddaughter was being treated at the Goldsboro Hospital's trauma center.

In order to keep the Clayton name out of the papers, and to suppress the fact that Edward had been drinking, Edward promised Slim a lot of money if he would remain silent about the crash and not contact the police, speak to the media, or report the accident to his insurance company. He told Slim that he would pay for all of Dakota's medical expenses, and would replace Slim's totaled Mustang, if Slim would go along with Edward's plan,

Slim, stunned and in severe shock about Dakota, agreed to Edward's terms and thanked him—anything to get off the phone and get to the hospital to see his granddaughter as quickly as possible.

At the hospital's trauma center, the chief surgeon, Dr. Daniel Kattrell Eickhoff, informed Slim and Lila about the extensive injures Dakota had sustained to her head and face, in addition to her many broken bones, and contusions throughout her body. He needed their consent to perform emergency surgery right away; setting her broken bones, removing shards of glass, stitching up many wounds, and stabilizing her vitals. Slim and Lila gave their consent immediately. The doctor added, that in addition, Dakota would need a lot of reconstructive surgery. But, he reassured them that in time her health and body would be restored back to normal.

Edward overheard Dr. Eickhoff's conversation with Slim and Lila. When the doctor walked away, Edward approached Slim and introduced himself, and handed over the papers he found in the Mustang. He expressed his concern about Slim's granddaughter and reiterated his previous offer to take care of all her medical expenses and get the best doctors money could buy, if they would keep silent about the accident. He told them that he would fly in the top plastic surgeons from Hollywood, and that Dakota would start a new life with a beautiful new face and stronger body. No one would ever know she had been in horrific crash. Slim, desperate to do anything to help save his beloved granddaughter, accepted Edward's offer again, knowing he could never afford to match it.

After enduring several months of grueling reconstructive surgeries, and suffering through the most excruciating pain her body had ever known, Dakota's bandages were ready to come off. Crowded into her hospital room were Lila, Slim, Edward, and the team of surgeons and nurses who had worked on Dakota. As Dr. Eickhoff slowly unraveled the bandages, he warned her that her face would still be swollen and may have some scars for a while. The room became still, and Dakota had butterflies in her stomach.

Finally, Dr. Eickhoff removed the last of the bandages and revealed Dakota's face. Everyone looked at Dakota with big smiles on their faces. Dakota grabbed the mirror from the nurse and looked at herself.

"Whoa, is that me? Oh my God! I'm beautiful."

She couldn't look away from the image in the mirror. She noticed that it was still her, but a thousand times better. Yes, her face was swollen but she couldn't even see the scars. She now had high sculpted cheekbones like those pretty models in the magazines. Her chin line was more defined, almost heart shaped. Her nose, which was okay before, was now thinner along the sides and more refined at the tip, almost upturned. Even her teeth were different. They seemed to be all perfectly matched and the brightest white she had ever seen. Her forehead must have been stretched upward, making her eyes seem almond shaped and more open and bluer.

"Wow!" she exclaimed, "You all did a great job! How can I ever thank you enough!"

She attempted to whistle, but her mouth was still sore. She was amazed though, that her mouth worked at all, after months of only eating and drinking food through a straw. Her lips seemed different too—thinner and more streamlined. She couldn't stop staring at herself.

Everyone was shaking hands and giving congratulatory slaps on the backs. Lila and Slim kept hugging Dakota and each other. They thanked Dr. Eickhoff and all of the doctors and nurses on the team who had worked tirelessly on Dakota and last but not least they thanked Edward, whose extreme generosity and dedication made all this happen for Dakota.

Dakota knew that someday she would pay a price for her total transformation. Grandpa Slim always told her, 'Dakota, we all have to pay a price for the things we want in life. There is no free ride.'

Dakota felt lucky to have Edward as her new friend. She felt close to him, but she knew it wasn't romantic in nature. That was for sure, since she was positive Edward didn't like girls.

Dakota woke up from her dream. She saw Edward sitting in her hospital room sipping a cup of coffee. Seeing him earlier must have triggered her memories about their crash and her surgeries so long ago.

She was still recuperating from Taylor's beating and Edward was still her best friend.

## CHAPTER TWENTY-SEVEN
# OFF TRACK

S ean bolted upright in his hotel bed wincing in pain. The clock read midnight. His injured left knee was throbbing. Making love in all contorted positions for hours on end didn't help. He glanced over at the leggy brunette next to him in bed. Francesca Jennings, his brother's executive assistant at his Wall Street investments company, looked at him and smiled. Sean had lost count of how many times he and Francesca had had sex. Francesca's athletic, acrobatic body had them both twisting all over the bed. Once they even crashed to the floor on top of each other while he was still climaxing inside her, probably scaring the hell out of the guests in their rooms below.

He couldn't get enough of her. She was older and much more sophisticated than Daniella and the young groupies he slept with. Funny, he recalled Francesca always being very cold and standoffish to him. She leaned over and rubbed her beautiful body over him again and again.

"What's wrong with you?"

"M-m my knee injury is acting up," he answered.

"Maybe you should get some ice to put on it."

"Y-you're right. I'll go and get some now."

Minutes later he was back. He sat on the edge of the bed and applied the ice to his knee. The cold sparked a memory. His stuttering kicked in big time. "Fr-Francesca, I almost forgot. Jimmy and I have to make an early morning guest appearance tomorrow in Lime Rock, Connecticut, for the All American Pro GT Race festivities. I-I better t-take you home now or put you in a cab. W-where do you live?"

She said, "That's okay, Sean. I can get my own cab. I'm staying with a friend since Lance and I split up."

When he and JP had flown up to New York City that morning to sign important tax papers at Connor's office, Sean and Francesca had flirted with each other and then made secret plans to meet at his hotel bar at 6:00 p.m.

Over drinks that evening, she confessed to Sean that she and her husband had split up. Francesca, came home unexpectedly early one day, and found Lance in bed with another man. Sean had said, "Jeez, you never really know the other person in your life."

Francesca lifted herself off Sean and dashed into the massive, all chrome, marble, and glass hotel shower, letting the water jets spray all over her very sore and achy body. As she lathered herself up with soap, she hoped "the kid" wouldn't make any trouble for her and Connor. She didn't need any hassles from the boss! "Kid" had always been her nickname for Sean.

It suddenly dawned on Sean that he was supposed to have called Daniella at 8 p.m. and it was now past midnight. *Damn,* he thought, *I'll have to call her.*

After Francesca left, Sean pulled out his cell phone. He noticed the battery was nearly discharged. Luckily he still had a little juice in it to call Daniella. She didn't answer, so he texted her: **Where r u?**" No reply. He called again and it went right to her voicemail. He said, "Where is she?"

Next, he called his twin sister.

"Hey, Avery, have you seen Daniella today?"

"No, bro, haven't seen her at all. Why?"

"I keep missing her, that's all."

"What's going on Sean? You're not doing the dirty with other girls again, are you? Oh, Sean, when will you learn?"

"Hey, I didn't say what I was doing. And what's up with you? You sound hyper, like when you were on stuff. Oh, no Av, you're not taking those diet pills again are you?"

The twins could always peer into each other's souls. Neither one answered the other one's question. They each hung up without another word. The weird guilty sensation between them was too much to ignore or respond to.

He texted JP: **Where have u been?**

JP texted back: **I'll call you.**

JP called and said, "Hey, Sean, let's meet down in the hotel's coffee shop say about 7:30 a.m. for an early breakfast so we can catch up on things before the limo picks us up for Lime Rock, okay?"

"Good idea," said Sean. "See you then. Take care, bro."

Sean was so exhausted from his all-night sex marathon, he fell into bed. Just before he dozed off, his last thought was to call Daniella again in the morning.

## CHAPTER TWENTY-EIGHT
## CHANGING LANES

H er call woke him out of a deep sleep. "Hullo," he said. "Who is this? Sean, is that you, boy? Where are you this time?"

"No, Billy Ray, this is Daniella. You know...Daniella Lawson. I'm calling from my apartment in South Beach. Sorry to call you so late."

"What time is it?"

"It's after midnight." she said in tears. "Sean was supposed to have called me tonight at 8:00, and I waited and waited to hear from him. I began to think the worst. He finally called me a few times a little while ago, but I was so upset, I didn't answer. You know, he and Jimmy had an appointment with Connor in New York City this morning. I was wondering if they spent the evening with Connor and Genji. Have you heard from him, Billy?"

"No, Daniella, I haven't heard from him, either. That's why I thought you were Sean, just now."

Billy Ray was used to Sean and Daniella going through many breakups and reconciliations. The trouble was always caused by Sean's fooling around all of the time. Billy Ray didn't want to come between his best friend and Daniella. He thought about calling Sean, but then changed his mind. After all, Daniella had been very upset and called him for help.

Billy Ray said to Daniella, "The boys have to be in Dover tomorrow in time for practice for the race that's coming up. Sean's not supposed to be running around with his bad knee. He'll never get out of that brace at the rate he's going. Enough about that. How are you doing, Daniella?"

"I can't sleep, Billy Ray. Do you mind if I drive up now and come and see you. I am so upset with Sean. I just need a shoulder to lean on, okay?"

Billy Ray looked at his watch, yawning. "Uh...yup, fine with me, Daniella, but are you sure you don't want to wait until you hear from Sean again? I'm sure he'll call you in the morning with a perfectly logical explanation."

"I just have a feeling he's up to no good again, Billy."

Billy Ray was thinking the same thing. "Would you like me to come and pick you up since it's so late? "

"No, thanks, Billy. I'm so worked up now, and I wouldn't be able to sleep anyway. I'll be okay.

Billy Ray asked Daniella if she had his address.

"Yes, I do, thanks," she answered.

"I'll put the coffee on. When you get here, bang on my door real hard, 'kay? Cuz I'll probably nod off. I'm not exactly a night owl," Billy Ray joked.

"Will do."

"Just drive safe. I don't want to worry about you, too," said Billy Ray.

"Billy, maybe you should take my cell number just in case."

"Wait a sec," he said. "Need to get a piece of paper and pen. Okay, shoot! What is it?"

He scribbled it down. *Hope I can read this back,* he thought when he hung up his phone.

Daniella was the total opposite of Dakota in so many ways. Although, Daniella was from New York City, a college girl, and a big-time marketing executive, she was always very down-to-earth and sincere whenever they met socially.

Dakota had put Billy Ray through emotional hell for the past several months. And then about a month ago, she walked out on him for good.

Billy Ray looked around his trailer and began to straighten up. He had lots of DVD's all strewn around and some clean laundry tossed around his bed. He hadn't had any visitors in a long time. He grabbed a quick shower.

Billy Ray put on the coffee maker and turned on the outside light. He tried waiting up for Daniella, but fell back into a deep sleep. It was 3:30 a.m. when he heard her loud knocking. He rubbed the sleep out of his eyes.

As soon as he opened the door to let Daniella in, Billy Ray knew he was in trouble. She was wearing white shorts and a frilly, gauzy top off one shoulder with a pretty pink bra peeping out. He was overcome by the scent of her expensive perfume.

She fell into his powerful arms, crying hysterically, "Oh Billy, I'm so unhappy and miserable. What am I going to do with Sean? He keeps breaking my heart."

He held her close for what seemed like a long time, and then they looked deeply into each other eyes and embraced. Her long copper red hair with spun gold highlights fell onto his shoulder.

"No, no, no, Daniella," he said. "We can't do this. We are betraying Sean." He tried to resist her but couldn't, and they shared a long and lingering kiss. Her green eyes reflected so much sadness and pain. He knew exactly what she was going through— having had his own heart ripped open by Dakota.

Billy Ray looked like he was poured into his jeans, revealing a great body, with muscles busting out all over. He was wearing a Devlin Motor Sports white tank top. His hair was still damp and his black curls danced around his head like a crown. His bulging biceps made Daniella's pulse quicken. She always knew he was attractive, but seeing how handsome he was up close, almost took her breath away. His face was a sculptor's dream, and his piercing black eyes looked right into her soul.

Caught up in the moment, they began tearing off their clothes and tumbled into his bed. Daniella's cell phone went off in the other room. She let it go to her voicemail. *Damn Sean, she thought, Let him rot.*

Naked and breathless, she and Billy Ray clung helplessly to each other.

Billy Ray had never been with someone like Daniella. She was so warm and sensuous, so different from Dakota. She had exquisite porcelain skin mixed in with some freckles. Her features and everything about her was delicate and fine. His mouth found her full breasts and as he caressed the curve of her hip, he felt himself lose control. His tongue discovered hidden places of pleasure as it traveled all over her exquisite body. As their bodies moved together in passion, he felt her pulsating wildly as they came together in ecstasy.

She caressed Billy Ray's powerful chest and then followed the design of a tattoo on his arm. Daniella wondered how Dakota could have walked out on such a beautiful and tender man.

He penetrated her again and again in a forceful but gentle way, almost as if he was erasing all traces of Sean. She moaned with pleasure. His thick thighs and tight round butt were so perfect. They fell asleep wrapped around each other.

She heard her cell phone go off again around 6:00 a.m., and although she hated to get out of Billy's bed, she decided to see if it was Sean and it was. Annoyed, Daniella ignored it. *Sean's a child compared to this magnificent man*, she thought. She got back into Billy's bed and put her phone on the nightstand, and like a bookmark, he hugged her close just like they were before. She stared into his handsome face and ran her fingers through his beautiful, black thick curls and once again collapsed into him with ravenous passion, kissing him all over. At that moment, Daniella made up her mind that no matter what, she was all through with Sean Chase Devlin.

She picked up her phone and texted Sean: It's all over, Sean. I don't want to be with you anymore! I have had enough. We are through! Then she tossed her phone on the carpeted floor and crawled back into Billy's arms.

The RV filled with the sun's early light. Billy Ray kissed Daniella good morning. They each knew something very special happened and didn't want their time together to end, but Daniella had to get back to work in South Beach and Billy Ray had to get to Dover to make preparations for the practice runs.

Daniella told him she had broken up with Sean for good this time via an earlier text. Over several cups of coffee they discussed their plans. They would have to proceed slowly. Once news got out about their relationship, there would be a lot of fallout that would have to be managed. They would have to take into consideration Sean's feelings, as well as the rest of the Devlins, and Billy Ray's teammates.

Billy Ray said, "This is not going to be easy, Daniella. I'm very concerned about Sean and how our relationship is going to hurt him?"

"Look, Billy," she said, "as far as I'm concerned Sean blew it big time with me. I gave him so many chances and he still couldn't remain faithful." Billy Ray said out loud, "I wonder if Sean will still want me to be his crew chief?" Daniella took his hand and held it tightly. She said, "You guys have been the hottest team in racing and the best of friends. I'm sure you'll both work it out."

Daniella whispered in Billy Ray's ear as she was leaving, "I'm willing to risk it and do whatever it takes, if you are." They shared a long goodbye kiss, so it would last until the next time they were together.

## CHAPTER TWENTY-NINE
# *360 DEGREES*

Jimmy Stanton was happy to be in New York City. The city always invigorated him, especially the financial district where he and Sean always stayed. He felt at ease as he blended in anonymously with the streams of people as they went about their daily rituals of wheeling and dealing in the world of high finance.

For some reason, Jimmy stopped having the terror-filled nightmares that had plagued him since his brutal kidnapping, a few weeks ago. He felt hopeful and he no longer had to put on a good front whenever he was around Sean and the Devlins.

When he was in detox right after his kidnapping, the therapist there taught him a trick to use whenever he had unpleasant thoughts. He told Jimmy to visualize a broom and to sweep away whatever had upset him. Just as Jimmy began to think about Sean's grandfather, Clayton, and how he might have had a hand in his kidnapping, Jimmy swept it out of his mind. The technique worked.

Jimmy couldn't stand to watch Sean cheating on Daniella. After overhearing Sean make private plans in Connor's office to meet Connor's assistant Francesca later, Jimmy decided to spend the whole day by himself at the Wynnley Casino in Atlantic City. Once there, he just hung out, people watched, and resisted the temptation to gamble. He had a great steak dinner and then went to see the exciting Cirque du Soleil show.

It was after midnight when the private limousine from Atlantic City, dropped Jimmy off at the boys' hotel on Wall Street. Jimmy had just finished his cell phone call to Sean. While he waited in the lobby for the elevator, he noticed a pretty girl standing next to him. The elevator door opened and the girl got on first, and Jimmy followed. They each pressed their floor buttons. It took him a few more seconds for her face to register with him, and then, *bam*, they both said at the same time, "Is that you, Jimmy?"

"Is that you, Katie? Katie McCall, what are you doing here?"

She still looked like a cute cheerleader—a pretty, slim, petite, brunette with a great smile. Sean, Katie, and Jimmy had attended Florida State University. He and Katie dated a short while and then lost touch when she got a job at a big bank in New York City and Jimmy began racing full time for Devlin Motor Sports.

Katie grinned, "My bank job just transferred me back to Miami. I had to give up my apartment here, so the bank is putting me up at this hotel while I finalize some last minute business transactions."

"Oh great!" Jimmy smiled back, and they exchanged contact information. As Jimmy handed Katie his DMS business card, he said, "I'll call you when I get back from Dover."

"You know, Jimmy," she said, as she held the door open when the elevator reached her floor, "I've been following your racing career, and I'm really happy you've been doing so well."

"Well, thank you, ma'am."

They both laughed, and each gave the other a peck on the cheek.

"See ya soon, Jimmy."

"Back-atcha," he said.

*Well that went well, Jimmy boy,* he thought. When he reached his floor and got out into the hallway, he whooped out loud, "Wh-hoo-wee! Well ain't that a kick in the ass!"

## CHAPTER THIRTY
# FLATLINED

D akota was still in the hospital recuperating from Taylor's beating. She wondered how Clayton was coming along. Dakota knew he was in the same hospital, but she hadn't been feeling well enough to visit him until now. She buzzed the nurses' station and was glad when the very sweet, young nurse, Maggie showed up. Dakota said, "Maggie, do you know what room Mr. Taylor Clayton Sr. is in?"

"Yes," she replied, "He's upstairs in the Neuro-Cardiac Intensive Care Unit."

"Maggie, do you think you could bring me up to see him? We're good friends. My wheelchair should be around somewhere."

"Well, uh, okay. There's a wheelchair out in the hallway. We'll have to be very careful. I don't want any trouble from the head nurse up there. Nurse Simmons, she's a tough one. I heard that Mrs. Devlin warned her about not allowing you near her father." Maggie asked, "Something bad happen between you two?"

"Please Maggie, I don't want to talk about it now, but as I mentioned before, Mr. Clayton and I are good friends. I'm sure he'll be happy to see me. Mrs. Devlin doesn't have to know, okay?"

"Well, Ms. Philips...," Maggie hesitated, "I'll come back later when Nurse Simmons goes off duty, and bring you up there. I'll wrap you in a blanket, so no one will see it's you, and hopefully you and I won't get caught."

A few hours later, Maggie, true to her word, came back with the wheelchair, and carefully helped Dakota into it. Dakota reached into her nightstand and took out a brush, mirror and lipstick and asked Maggie if she would help her with her hair. Dakota watched in her hand mirror as Maggie skillfully brushed her long hair and even applied her lipstick evenly. It was nice having Maggie around to help her.

"Gee, thanks so much Maggie. You did a great job."

She looked much better, despite the fact that her face was still black and blue and swollen. Her ribs were still very painful and sore.

Maggie covered Dakota with a blanket and wheeled her to the elevator. As soon as the elevator reached the Cardiac Intensive Care floor, Maggie pushed Dakota's wheelchair out and quickly found a secluded spot to park it. She called her friend at the front desk to find out if the coast was clear of any Devlins, and was told yes. Dakota lifted up her blanket and looked around for a minute. She got spooked by the eerie stillness and the hospital smells again. Her hands gripped the wheelchair arms so tightly her knuckles turned white. Maggie wheeled Dakota through the corridor doors to the exclusive area reserved for VIP's, The Mariella Clayton Wing, right into Clayton's private room. She removed Dakota's blanket.

Clayton had donated ten million dollars to the hospital many years before, in memory of his beloved wife.

"Maggie, this must be the wrong......" But then, Dakota looked more closely at the old man sleeping and realized it was Clayton. "Oh my God," she whispered. "He looks so old and frail."

He was hooked up to some monitors, an IV, tubes, and oxygen.

Dakota was crushed when all of her plans to defect to Villereal/ Clayton Racing collapsed because of Clayton's stroke. She had held out some hope that Clayton would rally. However, after seeing him the way he was now, she knew he wasn't going to make it.

Clayton opened his eyes when he heard something stirring in his room. He looked up. It took him a while to gather his thoughts and process who was there, but then he recognized Dakota. He became even more confused. *Why was she here and in a wheelchair?* Clayton's thoughts were jumbled lately. *Oh my God, it's really good to see her, but I'm so embarrassed for her to see me like this.* He pointed to his pad on the tray next to his bed, and she handed it to him. He scribbled down something with his good hand, "Wheelchair? Face? What happened to you?"

She replied, "Somehow Taylor found out about my swapping the flash drive, and when I bumped into her at your condo, she went berserk and kicked and punched the crap out of me. So, I'm here at the hospital, too."

He thought, *Oh God, I told Taylor to go get my 'Life Insurance' envelope but didn't think about the consequences.* He wrote, "So sorry." It took him a few minutes to write down each question he had for Dakota.

"Are you back with Billy? Who you driving for on Saturday?"

She answered, "I'm driving for your team. Taylor banned me from DMS."

Again he wrote, "Sorry." The tears fell down his face uncontrollably, and he felt so rotten and weak. But he was so happy to see her.

She told him, "I'm living in a hotel near your condo and no, I'm not back with Billy Ray. That's all over with," Dakota whispered.

Maggie rushed in to get Dakota and said, "We have to leave now, Ms. Philips. I think I saw Mrs. Devlin coming this way."

Dakota leaned out over her wheelchair, her ribs radiating a lot of pain and tried to hug Clayton tightly around his chest, avoiding all of his tubes and IV. Her own tears began to fall, and she couldn't control them. Maggie raced over to Dakota, covered her again with the blanket and whisked her away.

Dakota cried herself to sleep, not out of concern for Clayton, but for herself. She instinctively knew that her plans with Clayton were permanently shattered.

The next morning Maggie, the nurse, came to see Dakota. She had a funny look on her face. Dakota said, "What's wrong, Maggie? You look troubled."

"Well, Ms. Philips, I have some bad news, really bad news."

"Tell me, please."

"I found out from Nurse Simmons that Mr. Clayton died last night. His daughter, Mrs. Devlin was with him and so was his grandson, Sean Devlin. There was nothing anyone could do. His heart just gave out."

Dakota was getting used to disappointments.

## CHAPTER THIRTY-ONE
# RACING DAY AT DOVER

It was Saturday, the day of the Dover race. Once again Sean Devlin was the big-time favorite to win. The Devlin Motor Sports team was counting on it. The day started off sunny, hot, and humid with a few scattered clouds. Then, out of nowhere, along came flashes of lightning, thunder, and heavy rain which drenched the track. As if on cue, the sun came out again. Track officials sent out the powerful dryer trucks to blow the wet track dry for the race.

Earlier that morning, Sean had one of the expert trainers at the local gym give his knee a special treatment in their Jacuzzi. It helped him a great deal.

In the middle of all this, Sean missed Daniella. He kept thinking that maybe he'd win her back like all of the other times, despite her not responding to any of his many messages begging to see her. But right now, he had to focus on positioning his knee brace properly before the race.

The track was finally dried, and the drivers all climbed into their cars lined up in order on pit row.

Then the master of ceremonies made an announcement: "Ladies and gentlemen, on behalf of the Pro Motorsports Racing Association, we have a very sad announcement to make. The racing world has lost a great legend with the recent passing of Taylor Clayton Sr., co-owner of Villereal/Clayton Racing and VL Clayton Tobacco. Please, a moment of silence, as we honor this remarkable man who was a permanent fixture in stock car racing for over forty years. He will be greatly missed. Our prayers and sympathy go out to his family and team. There was a loud sound of awwws reverberating all throughout the grandstands. The VCR team had their caps over their hearts and said their silent prayers. The Devlin family wiped away their tears.

After the appropriate amount of time, the announcer then said the words all the fans waited so patiently to hear: "Drivers, start your engines!" The racing engines roared to life as the crowd screamed and cheered. The announcer declared, "It's the start of the Dover 300!"

Meanwhile, a TV anchor made an observation, "We'll sure be watching Sean Chase Devlin closely in the #17 car. If he wins this race today, he will break the Pro Motorsports Racing Association single-season victory record. By the way, his mother, former champion racer, Taylor Devlin, has come out of retirement to take over DMS's #23 car previously driven by Dakota Philips. Dakota Philips will be racing #42 car for her new bosses at Villereal/Clayton Racing."

Taylor's blood was boiling as she charged ahead in the #23 car. It burned Taylor that although her beloved father had died, Dakota was driving in one of Clayton's cars. It would be a tense race.

Everyone was fired up. Ace, Connor, Genji, Avery, Sekou, Hank, and guests cheered from the family's team pit box. Billy Ray and his #17 pit crew were at their best, making sure their driver was racing in optimum conditions—refueling, tire changing, and making adjustments in record speed.

Late in the race, Taylor pulled a move to block Dakota from advancing. She zoomed around Dakota's car and boxed her in while Sean and Jimmy took to the inside lane along with Carl Zimmer as they passed by to take the lead.

Suddenly Sean's car started to act sluggish and he began to lose power even though he had the throttle wide open. Jimmy wasted no time and passed Sean. Then Zimmer passed Sean and the rest of the pack started gaining on him. Billy Ray could hear Sean cursing and swearing over the radio. "Dammit, B-Billy, I'm losing power! I think there's something wrong with my f-fuel pump."

"Okay, Sean, you'll have to pit. We'll check it out," Billy Ray said calmly over the radio. He shared Sean's frustration as he continued to listen to him curse. Sean coasted his car to its stall on pit lane and the crew quickly went to work searching for the problem. It was bad news. They closed the hood on Sean's car and pushed it back to the garage. Sean Devlin was out of the race. He began screaming at the top of his lungs, "FUCK, FUCK, FUCK!"

Meanwhile, Jimmy Stanton showed off his incredible driving skills and continued to increase his lap times, as he pulled further ahead of the pack. Carl Zimmer held second place in Villereal/Clayton Racing's #41 car. He pursued Stanton as he dove into the curves to make time, but Jimmy kept increasing his distance, having the advantage of clean air while being in the lead. Taylor Devlin #23 car held tight to an impressive third place, frustrating Dakota Philips' #42 car's efforts to pass her. The fans were blown away by Taylor's kicking butt and racing like the pro she used to be. It was hard for anyone to believe she hadn't raced in many years.

The yellow caution flag suddenly came out on the two hundred ninety-eighth lap. The officials halted the race for debris on the track. The pace car pulled out ahead of the pack and Jimmy lost his lead only two laps before the finish lap. All the race cars were packed together in a double row according to track position before the race was halted. It was going to be a green-white-checkered finish. Tension mounted. Now it was anybody's race. Stanton and Zimmer were cruising side-by-side behind the pace car. Jimmy chose the inside lane.

Finally the debris was cleared and the pace car exited the track. Stanton and Zimmer were at the head of the pack. The green flag was out and the roaring energy of the speeding cars reached a crescendo. The fans stood up, cheering and waving their arms as the speeding cars dove into turn one. Stanton and Zimmer, still side-by-side, accelerated out of turn two. Zimmer floored it, hoping to get past Stanton when his tires suddenly slipped on the pavement. Stanton inched ahead and Zimmer changed lanes hoping to get better traction. The maneuver worked and Zimmer was right on Stanton's rear bumper. The white flag came out. It was now or never for Zimmer. He tried to pass Stanton in the outside lane, but Jimmy blocked him and held his lead. It was the final lap. Zimmer managed to pull up on the outside lane but Stanton had the stronger car. The pack roared to the finish line as Jimmy's car was just a bumper ahead of Zimmer's. The crowd went wild as Jimmy Stanton crossed the finish line to win his first Dover 300.

In the winner's circle, Jimmy told Sean how sorry he was for him that he didn't get the chance to break the single-season victory record. Sean frowned and answered sharply, "Yeah, it sucked big time," but quickly caught himself and said, "Hey, Jimmy there'll be another day for that. Today was your day, bro." Then he grinned as Jimmy was catapulted onto the crew's shoulders. Champagne bottles were popping and Jimmy and Billy Ray and the crew were drenched in champagne. Sean scanned the roaring crowds to see if he could catch a glimpse of Daniella, but there was no sign of her.

## CHAPTER THIRTY-TWO
## *FAMILY MATTERS*

A ce called Benecio Villereal and asked him to please meet him at McLeod's Tavern, a local racing hangout in Dover, at 8 p.m.

The purpose of his meeting with Villereal was a very important one. You might say it was going to be a life-changer, big time. Ace needed a drink to steady his hands. He caught the bartender's eye and ordered a shot of bourbon.

Before he knew it, Villereal came strutting towards him. *God, he still looked good, the ole bugger. Not one gray hair,* Ace thought to himself as he stroked his own mane, now all silver on both sets of his sideburns. *Well, Benecio didn't have kids,* and then he stopped himself.

Never far from Ace's thoughts was the investigation into his best friend Benecio's possible involvement in Jimmy's kidnapping, but that was a matter for another time. Right now, Ace had to help him get through one of the most important events of his life.

"So Ace, my man," Benecio said as he greeted Ace with a handshake and a pat on the back. "What's with all of the cloak and dagger stuff? I thought we left all of that back in the Gulf War."

"Benecio, I think you should have a drink first. What'll you have?"

Benecio glanced over to the bartender. "Scotch and soda." He sat down in the chair next to Ace and said, "You look like crap! What's bugging you?"

Ace's heart was pounding a little too fast and hoped he didn't drop dead before he delivered the news to Benecio. He turned and looked at his friend squarely in the eyes. "Okay Benecio, what I have to show you will blow your mind, but first, I want you to promise me that you will not shoot the messenger. Promise me!"

"Okay, okay. I will not shoot you." Benecio's face started to pale a little. "Ace, you're scaring me. Are you dying?" Then wide-eyed he joked, "Am I dying?" Ace took a moment to gather his thoughts when Benecio piped up and asked, "By the way, I am so blown away by Clayton's death. I still can't believe it. He was like a father to me. The whole team is in shock. How is Taylor and the family handling it?"

Ace said, "Benecio, do you mind if we talk about that later? I have something else to show you that's very important.

"Oh, okay Ace. Sure, no problem. Please, go ahead."

Ace's hand shook as he took out the envelope and handed it to Benecio. His heart began to race again. Benecio looked at the address on the envelope and the return address and had a blank expression on his face. Inside the envelope were two documents. He read them both carefully and then, he started to cry. It was such an emotionally charged moment for Benecio that Ace wished he had found them a much more private place. He felt for his pal and didn't know what to do to help.

"Benecio, Taylor showed me these papers a few weeks back. I am still in shock and you must understand how difficult this has been for me trying to figure out a way to tell you. Taylor didn't take this news very well. I'd keep far away from her if I were you."

Benecio kept staring at the birth certificate in disbelief. There in print was his name listed as the biological father of a baby boy. The second certificate stated that the baby boy had been adopted by Michael and Ann Harper. Benecio was full of so many mixed emotions and questions.

"Ace, is this the same Billy Ray Harper as your crew chief?"

Ace nodded.

"How did you get these documents? Who had them? Why now?"

"They were among Clayton's papers."

Benecio fell silent for a moment and then said, "Ace, I need to get out of here."

"Okay Benecio, I'll go wherever you want."

Then Benecio said, "I want to see Billy Ray. Let's go to his place."

Once they got outside, Ace called Billy Ray. Benecio listened to Ace's side of the conversation: "Hi, Billy Ray. It's me, Ace. I know it's late and you must be busy, but would you mind if Benecio Villereal and I came ovah to see you now? We have something very important to discuss with you.... No, not to worry Billy. It has nothing to do with your job. You're doing great as always! Yes, it is terrible that Clayton passed way. Thank you. I'll pass along your condolences to Taylor and the family. So it's okay if we come ovah? It's kind of important.... Oh, great. We're at McLeod's. Your RV is parked near the track right? It should take us about twenty minutes.... Great! See you in a bit, Billy, and thanks!"

Benecio paced back and forth, not knowing what he would say to Billy Ray. He found it ironic that he and his son had both been involved in racing and in close proximity for several years.

He started toward his car and said, "Okay, I'm ready to meet my son!"

**WHEN ACE KNOCKED** on Billy Ray's RV, Villereal thought his heart would burst. This was going to be harder for him than he thought.

Billy Ray opened the door and stared at them as they stood in the dark.

Ace said, "Hey, Billy!"

Billy Ray said, Hey guys! Please, come on in."

He was glad that he had cleaned up his place and made himself look presentable. He wished that Daniella was with him for support, but knew it wasn't the right time to rub their relationship in Ace's face.

Villereal never had a reason before to take a close look at Billy Ray. His eyes remained locked on his son, and for the first time he noticed the strong resemblance they both shared.

Billy Ray invited them to sit down, and handed out beers. After making small talk, Billy Ray hoped they'd get right down to business. The suspense was killing him.

Ace finally said, "Well, son, you're probably wondering why we're here. We have uncovered some very important information that pertains to you personally."

"What information, Ace?"

"Okay, Billy Ray. Here goes. When Clayton was still alive and in the hospital, he had Taylor retrieve some important documents for him that were stored in his condo." Ace sighed and said to Villereal, "Please give him the envelope to read, Benecio." Then he continued. "These were among them."

"What documents?" said Billy Ray as he reached for the envelope.

Ace said, "Maybe you should have some of that beer first."

Billy Ray began to feel light-headed. He took a sip of beer and put the cold bottle against his forehead. His hand shook after he took the envelope from Villereal. Finally, he'd find out what was going on.

Billy Ray began to read the first document, and Villereal could see it was the copy of his birth certificate. He then read the second one. Billy Ray's eyes began to tear up. So many questions raced through his mind. He asked both men," Why did Clayton have my documents? Why wasn't I told this before?"

Billy Ray was overcome with emotion. He asked, "Benecio, how did you meet my mother?"

Villereal reached for his wallet and pulled out a faded photograph and handed it to Billy Ray. It was a picture of a beautiful young girl. Villereal responded in a trembling voice, "It was a long time ago. This was your mother, Rosalinda. I loved her very much."

Billy Ray stared at the photograph intently. Finally he stood up and said, "We have a lot to talk about Benecio, but it's too much for me to deal with now. Please leave. I have to be alone."

Ace and Villereal walked out of the RV.

## CHAPTER THIRTY-THREE
# *RICOCHET*

Dakota had always had her life all planned out, but now, everything was up in the air. Dakota was restless. She was still living at the hotel. Her nasty black and blue marks were finally fading. It was time for her to make new plans.

Dakota hoped she could be restored to a position of power at Villereal/Clayton Racing. Her plan was to exploit her relationship with Benecio Villereal. She was very fortunate to be driving for VCR, since she had been permanently blackballed from Devlin Motor Sports.

Dakota texted Benecio and asked to meet with him to discuss her driving maneuvers for their upcoming races. He texted her back: Sure. Come over to my house. Come in forty-five minutes.

His house wasn't too far from the hotel. Although Taylor had been covering for her father temporarily at Villereal/Clayton Racing while Clayton was still recuperating, now that he was dead, Benecio was running the day-to-day operations.

All of the lights were on in Benecio's house. Although she had been to his house many times, she still felt its creepy vibes. Maybe it was the overgrown trees and shrubs, but it always appeared to be hiding secrets. She knocked on the front door. Benecio got up right away, ran his hand through his hair, and opened the front door. The look in his eyes told her she had made a huge mistake in coming there.

"Come in," he said as he motioned with his hand. "How are you feeling? You still look badly bruised."

She responded, "Thanks, I'll be all right."

She realized that she would not be able to use her charms on him.

He showed her to the living room.

"Would you like something to drink? Wine, perhaps?" he asked, as he pulled a bottle of wine from the wine rack.

"Wine would be fine," she said feeling a little more relaxed. She sat down in one of the leather and chrome, black chairs. Benecio handed her a glass of wine.

Villereal stepped over to his desk and opened a drawer to retrieve a bag.

He said, "Dakota, I have some things I need to discuss with you." With that Benecio took something out of the bag.

She recognized Sean's original #17 flash drive, the one that she had removed from his race car right before the Triax 400. She gritted her teeth. *Oh God! It's all over for me. I'm ruined,* she thought. *This wasn't adding up? How did Taylor find out about the defective flash drive and how did she get hold of it? How did anyone find it when it had been in my purse and then hidden away in my luggage?*

Villereal spoke up, "Dakota, I've given this a lot of thought. Your power-hungry, criminal behavior cost you your job at Devlin Motor Sports. You're so damn lucky Ace didn't have you arrested." Villereal walked over with the bag and stood in front of Dakota. He said, "I'd always be looking over my shoulder, wondering when you'd start with your treachery and dirty tricks at VCR, and since I cannot ignore your past misdeeds. I'm taking this evidence to PMRA and let them decide whether you have a future in professional racing. As far as I am concerned, your racing career is over. You don't have Clayton to lean on for protection anymore."

Dakota, shocked and enraged all at once, said, "But wait, Benecio, I thought we had a future. All those times we were together and made plans to sabotage the Devlins. To quote your exact words you sonuvabitch: 'I'm getting back what Ace robbed from me: Taylor. If I couldn't have her, then I didn't want anyone else to have her, especially Ace." Dakota continued, "Benecio, *you* were the one who set the plan into action, not Clayton. He was just a pawn in your scheme to take down the Devlins, and take down Clayton, too.

So then, you would have full control of Villereal Racing. It was you who helped me get Sean and Jimmy out of the way. Was all of our lovemaking just a lie to you?"

"Yes," said Villereal. "You don't think I could ever care for someone as ruthless and cunning as you, someone who could destroy her own teammates just to get ahead?"

"Aren't you doing the same thing, Benecio?" she said.

"Yes, but I earned it!"

Dakota felt like she was going to explode. She screamed, "Okay, Benecio, I'm out of here! Once I leave, you won't have me anymore for your team. Just think of that! Who are you going to get to fill in for me?"

"Oh," he said, "I already hired Zimmer's son, Ricky. He's been breaking records in the National Series. I'm sure you've heard of him."

Dakota jumped up and with clenched fists was about to strike him hard in the face, but Villereal reacted quickly and pushed her back down into her seat.

"You know Dakota, there'll always be someone who is better than you just waiting in the wings to beat your record. Are you going to wipe out every challenger you have? Believe it or not, Ricky has made it the right way, on his own merits, without any games. You couldn't even face the fact that your teammates, Sean and Jimmy, are great racers, too."

"What if I tell PMRA about your involvement?" said Dakota.

"They wouldn't believe you," said Benecio, "and once I show them the damning evidence of your flash drive, you're toast. NOW GET THE HELL OUT OF HERE!"

Dakota reached for her bag and was going to make a run for the front door, when Villereal said "Oh, just one more thing, Dakota. I wanted to commend you on the great research you did for Billy Ray."

"Huh?" she said, turning around to face him.

Shoving a copy of the birth certificate that Ace had given him in front of her face, Villereal declared, "I wanted to thank you for finding out who Billy Ray's biological father is. As you can see, it's *me*! If you had played your cards right, I could have been your future father-in-law!" Devastated, Dakota ran to the front door and yelled, "This isn't over!" And she escaped out into the night.

## CHAPTER THIRTY-FOUR
# CAN A LEOPARD CHANGE HIS SPOTS?

It had been three weeks since the Dover race, and no one had heard from Sean. He missed two races. He wasn't taking any phone calls either. Jimmy figured that Sean was in bad shape. First, it was Daniella's surprise break up with him, and then there was the shock of his grandfather's death, which had left many unanswered questions. And then the final blow, Daniella had left him for Billy Ray.

Jimmy couldn't imagine what Sean was going through, and he was angry with himself for not speaking up sooner after observing his best friend being unfaithful to Daniella time after time. It was like watching a runaway train. The sad thing was, Sean wouldn't have listened to Jimmy anyway.

Jimmy's phone rang. To his great surprise, it was Sean who invited him to meet at their private spot at Ormond Beach. Sean said, "I need to discuss some things with you."

They had been meeting at their private spot since they were teenagers, where they surfed, drank beer, took walks along the shore, and talked about girls.

It was a very pleasant March morning, clear without the usual humidity. The boys greeted each other with their usual hi-five hand slaps, and then Sean grabbed hold of Jimmy and just hugged him for a long time. Finally, Sean turned away and wiped the tears from his eyes. He grabbed a bag and pulled out a couple of cold beers and handed one to Jimmy. Sean forced a grin on his face and as they clinked their bottles,

Sean made a toast. "To better times!" Jimmy responded, "And to good friends!" They both looked out into the calm ocean and watched the sunrise as they drank. Sean looked very pale and even with his sunglasses on, Jimmy could tell Sean had dark circles under his eyes,

Finally Sean spoke. "I guess you want to know why I wanted to meet."

Jimmy, still staring out on the water, didn't look at him. "Okay, why did you want to meet?"

"Well, I feel like shit! I know I am totally to blame for ruining it with Daniella by screwing around. I knew damn well what the consequences would be, but I did it anyway. I couldn't help myself. I don't know why I keep cheating. Do you?"

Jimmy looked at him and grinned, "Sure! You're Sean Devlin, every chick's dream! You're not happy until you've nailed every female that comes your way!"

Sean hated hearing those words from Jimmy, even though he knew it was the truth. Pissed, he smashed his beer bottle hard against some rocks perched along the beach, and reached for a new one. As he opened it, he turned to Jimmy and said, "Did you have to be so honest?"

"The truth hurts, don't it, Devlin. Sorry. Maybe I shouldn't have been so blunt, but I had to tell you how I feel! That's what friends do."

Sean was silent for a while, lost in deep thought. Then he said, "Bad enough I lost Daniella, but I lost her to Billy Ray!" His voiced cracked, "B-Billy Ray! Of all people, why did it have to be him?"

Jimmy gripped Sean's shoulder. "Come on, bud, take it easy."

Sean pushed him away and stared at him. Then he chuckled sarcastically, "Talk about feeling w-weird? It can't be easy for them either. Luckily, my p-parents are caught up in mourning for my grandfather. They'll probably f-freak out when they find out what's been going on."

Jimmy shook his head and took another swallow of beer. Sean kicked up some sand and continued to drown himself in self-pity.

Sean said to JP, "The t-truth is I just can't accept that it's p-permanently over with Daniella. In my heart, I know I have lost her for good, but I just can't grasp the reality of it."

"Why not, Sean? What can't you grasp? Did you really think you could get away with fooling around with the likes of the Francesca's of the world and not get caught?"

"I kinda been thinkin'..." Sean frowned with a new determination. "I have d-decided to become a b-better person by trying to figure out why I c-cheat. If I can understand the *whys*, then maybe I can find a way to control it. I am not p-proud of being such a jerk. It's just something I've been doing for so long, and the p-pity of it is, I never f-feel any remorse or guilt, and I still end up feeling empty inside. I'm not going to go all Freudian on you, but I'm sure it has s-something to do with my g-goddamn s-stutter and my m-my-god awful mother."

"Holy shit, Sean. You really mean that?"

"Mothers always get blamed, but in my case my m-mom was ashamed of me and my stutter, so she did everything in her p-power to wipe it out of me. As if I could control it. I'm probably afraid of getting too close to women, cuz deep down, if any woman got to know me, they'd see my flaws—mainly my stutter. I do owe her a lot though—for teaching me to race cars and for instilling in me a love for speed and the guts to always push the limit."

Jimmy saw that Sean's eyes were tearing up again, so he just let him talk.

"Here I am," said Sean all choked up, "still standing, lucky to be alive, and lucky to still be racing and still luckier to have a great family and a friend like you, JP." They clutched hands and shook them like old friends.

Sean smiled and looked at the foaming surf. Suddenly he yelled, "Even though my dad thinks a leopard can never change his spots, I'm here to tell you he's full of shit! This leopard *will* change! YEE-HA!" He ripped off his shirt and raced into the ocean. Jimmy grinned and dove in after him, and they swam through the waves and rode the surf in the morning sun.

## CHAPTER THIRTY-FIVE
# TAYLOR'S NIGHTMARES

Seventeen year old Taylor Clayton felt as if she was soaring high overhead peering down over the horrific wreckage of a sports car. She could see her clothes all spattered in blood. The smell of death was in the air. Her hands were dripping with blood! She looked over at the nearby tree where the bloodied broken body of a young woman lay crumpled and motionless. She saw herself run over to the lifeless body and cradle it close.

In shock, she screamed, "NO-O-O-O! Rosalinda! Rosalinda, wake up! WAKE UP! You can't be dead! You can't do this to me! Please wake up!" In tears, she cried out, "I never meant for this to happen to you! I was only trying to scare you. You took my Benecio away from me. I love him so."

Taylor, still looking down, heard herself saying, "Now you'll never get in my way again! Benecio belongs to ME! He's mine, do you hear me?"

Partially awake now, she turned around and reached out into the darkness. She felt the embrace of the cold and she began to shiver uncontrollably. She screamed out into the darkness, "Daddy, oh Daddy! I'm so scared. DADDY! Please help me! Da..."

Ace shook his wife awake. "Taylor, sweetheart, wake up! You are having another nightmare."

Ace had never witnessed his wife having them before. Her screaming woke him out of a deep sleep.

He tried to make sense out of what she was saying, "Stop! Look out! Oh no, I have to turn now. Turn now! Oh, no, that car is coming straight at me! Won't make it... won't make it! Rosalinda! Rosalinda!"

It was becoming more difficult to calm her down. When Ace asked her about her nightmare the next morning she told him she had no recollection and didn't understand what he was talking about.

Ace recalled the name Rosalinda. His curiosity got the best of him. He needed to know what was tormenting his wife in her sleep. Over lunch one day in the city, he decided to ask his brother-in-law Edward Clayton some questions about Taylor's past.

Ace asked, "Was Taylor ever violent?"

"Not really. Maybe a little," Edward said. "She used to hit me if she felt like it. But wait—I do recall something bad happened when she was about seventeen. I don't know exactly, but Dad paid off people to hush something up that she did."

Ace would have to look into this more deeply, especially if it was related to Taylor's nightmares.

"Do you remember someone named Rosalinda?"

"Wait a minute, Edward said. "When we were kids, we had a maid Bonita who watched over Taylor. My spoiled sister was a handful. Bonita used to bring her niece, umm, Rosalinda-something, to work with her. Her niece was visiting from Mexico that summer. Yes, now I remember... She was very beautiful and Benecio seemed to fall for her, too. That didn't sit well with my jealous sister. Rosalinda was there to help her aunt but never really did. She was more interested in sneaking off with Benecio."

Then the name Rosalinda struck Ace like a bolt of lightning! It was on Billy Ray Harper's birth certificate along with Benecio Villereal's name as the birth father.

Edward said, "Ace, you might want to discuss all this with Benecio. I don't mean to make this even more awkward for you but they were so close then."

Ace was puzzled since he had never known Taylor to have a violent side until now, when he saw how she had brutally assaulted Dakota Philips. She kept saying something about her driving in her nightmares. Ace decided that no matter what he would find out about his wife's past, he would always stick by her.

Photo by Mitchel Gray

## ABOUT THE AUTHOR

**JOANNA LEE DOSTER** is a writer and author whose previously published work includes Celebrity Bedroom Retreats and a series of nationally syndicated celebrity profiles that featured legendary sports figures. She is a freelance journalist for syndicated newspapers, magazines and blogs. In addition, she has held executive positions in cable television, communications and the entertainment industry. She and her husband live in New York.

www.ingramcontent.com/pod-product-compliance
Lightning Source LLC
Chambersburg PA
CBHW020131180626
46810CB00004B/1496